SAVED
BY THE WOLF

THE MCCULLOUGH PACK BOOK 1

NOLA LI BARR

Tapioca Press

This is a work of fiction. Names, characters, places, and incidents either are the products of the author's imagination or are used fictitiously. Any resemblance to actual persons, living or dead, events, or locales is entirely coincidental.

Edited by Corina Douglas, Burning Legacies Publishing
Cover design by Artscandare Book Cover Design

ISBN 978-1-956919-42-4 (paperback)

www.nolalibarr.com

Free Book Offer

Meet the parents that started the McCullough Pack. Receive a FREE copy of *Rescued by the Wolf* when you join Nola's newsletter. Be the first to know about new releases and giveaways.

newsletter.nolalibarr.com/mcculloughpack

About this Book

Jill

His voice connects with something deep inside of me, and all I want is to be in his arms.

But the bruises from my last relationship have only just healed, and the way his friends follow his every command reminds me too much of my ex.

And yet, there's something about him that calls to me. He's the one my heart demands . . . .

Luc

She's timid and shy, and even though she's human, my wolf is drawn to her. He's the happiest when I'm next to her and wants me to claim her as my own.

But after my last relationship, I have sworn off love, and the last thing I want is to be hurt again.

Yet, no matter my reasons, my wolf just won't let go . . . .

McCullough Pack

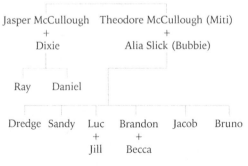

JILL

"HERE'S TO A NEW LIFE, a new beginning, and a new start! To Jill!" Becca yelled from the top of the mountain.

It wasn't really a mountain, per se. Really, it was just a hill, but it was the tallest one we could find on short notice. Up here, I felt like the queen of the world, and for the first time in a long time, I felt free.

"I'm scared, though," I admitted to Becca.

"I know, sweetheart, but you deserve your freedom. You've had a horrible time. You know I've been trying to get you to break up with Wolfhound—or whatever he wants to be called these days—for the last two years. Now you've finally done it!"

"He wasn't happy when I told him I wasn't coming back. And his name's Rich; only his goons call him Wolfhound," I said, picking at my nails. They were chewed down to the skin; something Rich hated.

He was always on my case to take better care of myself—and not in the health department, but in the beauty department. He needed me as eye candy to impress his boys. My black hair and Taiwanese exotic looks made other people jealous, and Rich fed off that.

He had been charming at the beginning, taking care of my every need. It wasn't until I moved into his place that he started being more controlling, showing more of who he really was. But by then, I couldn't have escaped, even if I wanted to.

"If it wasn't for you, I'd still be with him," I said, looking up at Becca.

She put her arm around me. "But you're not, and you're never going back to him," she said firmly.

"How did you do it, anyway? When I told him I wasn't coming back yesterday, he just let me walk out of his place. Not one of his goons held me back. I was shaking all the way to my car, and even on the drive here."

"I'm a lawyer, and I did some magic," Becca said simply. "That's all I'm going to say." But her smirk said otherwise.

"You've got dirt on him, don't you?"

"I can't say." Becca ran her hands through her bright red hair, then released a deep sigh. "I just don't want to get you involved. The key right now is starting your life again."

"All right," I replied, able to see that she really did want the best for me. And after what she'd done to help me escape, it was the least I could do.

She gestured at the view, abruptly changing the subject. "You got enough fresh air? It's getting chilly up here. I say we pack up this picnic and head back to the hotel where we can watch some episodes of Friends."

I nodded eagerly. "That sounds like a great plan."

"And tomorrow, we'll meet with Brandon to look at a brand new place for you to start over."

My heart raced with a mixture of nerves and excitement. "I hope Brandon knows I'm so thankful for what he's done for me."

"Sweetheart, he knows. Brandon and I kick butt in the courtroom. He was as invested in getting you out as I was."

"But to also offer me a place in his family's complex, way out from the city? That's generous, Becca."

She nodded. "Yes, but it'll be a nice fresh start for you. It's a small, quiet town—but not too small—and you'll be free to go wherever you want. Just be sure to let me know if you have any issues; although, that's highly unlikely as Brandon's family owns the town. Oh, and by the way, I talked to Ray, Brandon's cousin, and she's excited to have you come and work with her at her floral shop."

My jaw dropped. *I had a job already?* "Oh wow, that's fantastic!" Then reality hit me, and I felt tears prick my eyes. "I can't believe this. Not being locked in Rich's place all day is going to take some getting used to. If you weren't already my friend before I met him, and if you didn't help me get out, I might have never seen another human again! Thank you, Becca."

Becca pulled me into her arms and gave me a tight squeeze. "You're going to be all right, Jill. I know it."

"I hope so," I mumbled, holding onto her tightly.

After a minute, Becca whispered into my ear. "It's your turn to yell."

I looked up at her with watery eyes and smiled. "You're going to tell me it's cathartic, right?"

"It sure is, and you know I'm not going to let you leave until you do." Smiling, Becca turned me around to look at the view of my new home.

I squeezed her hand as I took in the sight, took a deep breath, and yelled out, "To my new life! To my new beginning! To me!" I was huffing by the last word but felt a small glimpse of hope worming its way into my heart.

"It's good to see a genuine smile on your face again," Becca said, hooking her arm through mine as we walked back to her car.

"Becca, this is really nice," I said in awe, eying the apartment complex in front of me. It looked like a ski lodge on the end of Main Street. At four stories tall, it looked so cosy nestled into the surrounding forest.

"Yeah, it's even nicer than Brandon described it."

We both stood there in awe of my new home for a moment before I turned to Becca and asked her, "You know what's even more awesome?"

Becca inclined her head to let me know she was listening.

"I'm not only within walking distance to the florist, but also the bakery where I saw your favorite carrot cake sandwich!"

"Really?" Becca's head whipped around so fast that I burst out laughing. Her face softened. "It's so nice to hear you laughing, Jill."

I hooked my arm through Becca's and pulled her into the lobby. A big, open fireplace sat in the middle of the room, sofas and chairs surrounding it. The rental office was to the left, and an older woman with curly white hair, librarian glasses, and a sweet smile was staring back at me.

"Hi, I'm Becca, and this is Jill," Becca announced to the woman. "Brandon McCullough said he had a room for Jill here."

"Yes, I've been waiting for you," she said, a warm smile spreading across her face as she looked at me. I didn't know why, but it felt like I had come home. Before I could dive deeper into the feeling, the old lady continued, "My name is Miti, and I'll be showing you to your room. It has a fantastic view; you'll love it. Come with me."

She grabbed the keys on the table in front of her, and we followed her to the elevators and up to the fourth floor. The doors opened into a dark hallway. The carpet was a deep red with a well-worn path down the middle, and the walls were black. Mini chandeliers hung from the ceiling, lighting up the hallway and providing an elegant ambiance. The doors on each unit were solid wood, with black knobs and knockers.

The decor was the exact opposite of Rich's unit, where everything looked white and shiny and pristine—as if nothing bad could ever happen there. I smiled at the refreshing change and took in a deep breath. Becca squeezed my hands, as if aware I was starting to let go of my old life.

The old lady beckoned us to follow. "It's at the end of the hallway," she said over her shoulder. "There are staircases next to your unit, but the only elevator is the one we just came up in."

"I heard howling last night from our hotel," Becca said. "Does that happen often? Are there wolves here?"

"Becca, I'm sure everything's fine." I didn't want to hear about any concerns. Brandon was doing me a solid by letting me stay in his family's apartment for a discounted rate. I could afford to live here and still save money. Plus, the floral shop was only a ten-minute walk away.

"Yes, there are wolves here," the old lady said. "But I wouldn't worry about them. I've lived here for thirty years and never had any problems. Safe as can be. As for the howling, earplugs work wonders; I sleep with them in every night, and I don't hear a thing."

The old lady kept rattling on about the good traits of the building and town, both of which sounded safe enough. Besides, nothing could be worse than what I had been living through. I was already sold.

We heard the elevator ding behind us and turned to see three burly men walk out. My heart rate spiked, and I felt Becca grab my arm to steady me. Her grip was so hard that I knew she was as affected by the men as I was. Handsome didn't begin to describe them, but the similarity in their build was just like Rich's, and I could feel my knees buckling underneath me.

Strong arms steadied me and drew me back up into a standing position. I looked up, thinking Becca had come around to stand in front of me, only to see a set of dark brown eyes boring into mine. My first reaction was to bolt and hide behind Becca, but the attraction I had for this man was so strong that I couldn't look away. *Where were these feelings coming from? I'd never had such strong feelings for Rich, and I didn't even know this man!*

Regardless of my confusion, my body stayed rooted to the spot, as if intuitively knowing I was safe with him. His smell was intoxicating, nothing like Rich's gluttony of perfumes. This man smelt like the forest air, clean and simple. It was all I could do to not lean in and actively inhale his scent. Add in his strong, bulky shoulders and steel-cut arms, and I could feel a ripple of fire arrowing to my core.

"Are you okay?" he asked me.

It was a true baritone voice, one that sent my insides squirming. I could only stare back at him. Vaguely, I heard Becca echo his question. My head slowly turned to Becca, and her worried face snapped me out of my daze.

"I'm okay!" I shot back. "I'm fine. Really, I am. I don't know what came over me." I shrugged off the man's hands and backed up, clenching Becca's arm instead.

His eyebrows were still furrowed, and I wanted to reach up and smooth them out. No one that handsome should have worry lines, especially about me.

"If you say so," was all he said before turning to the old lady.

"Miti, is there anything we can help you with?" he asked her.

"This young lady came to see Unit 423."

His eyebrows shot up. "What about the other—?"

Miti cut him off with a stern look. "Brandon was adamant that a room with a calming view was necessary. I believe she'll like it. We'll soon have the place filled."

Shock crossed the man's features for a split second, but he quickly covered it up with a neutral expression, leaving me curious as to what he was thinking. "Well, we won't keep you from seeing your room," he replied, turning back to face me. "I'm Luc, and this is Damon and Brent. We live down the hall, so just let us know if you ever need any help."

"Thanks," I said, conscious I was still gawking and trying not to.

They left us standing in the hallway as they retreated into their units. Miti didn't seem fazed by their appearance. She turned and continued walking, expecting us to follow. We did, and I tried my best to ignore the odd look Becca was giving me.

"Here we are, Unit 423," Miti announced in front of one of the doors.

She rattled the key in the lock before it clicked, but the door opened without a sound into a brightly lit room with a view to die for. I instantly gravitated to the ceiling-to-floor window that overlooked the forest as far as the eye could see. I drew in a breath that I hadn't realized I was holding. I had missed being surrounded by all these trees. My childhood memories were filled with fun times in the woods spent jumping creeks, swinging on ropes, and swimming in the lake. If my parents were still alive, they would have loved this view.

"The view is something else," Becca said, repeating what was in my mind. "I took a look at the kitchen and bathroom, and everything looks to be spotless and in working order."

"I like it here," I whispered.

"Especially with the hunks down the hallway."

"Yeah . . ." I said without thinking. Then I shot her a look.

"Don't take it that means I'm moving on. I'm off guys for the moment. It's time to focus on myself for a while."

"It's okay to still look, though," Becca said with a knowing look. "You were clearly taken in by Luc." She nudged my shoulder, and I could feel a blush forming on my cheeks.

"Quiet," I hissed. "Miti is here."

Becca shrugged. "I have a feeling she's not fazed by anything."

"Well, I'd like to at least pretend to keep these thoughts to ourselves."

"As you wish," Becca said, smiling. "But I do think this is the place for you. You look happy, and as you said before, you can afford this place and be able to save up for your new life."

"Yes, I agree." I turned back to Miti, who had just walked up behind us. "I'll take it. This is exactly what I'm looking for."

Her face broke out in a smile. "Great! I think you'll like it here. Just remember to get a set of earplugs."

LUC

"WHY THAT APARTMENT!" I threw a plate across the room, satisfied at the sound of it shattering against the wall. The aroma of baked lasagna was wafting from the oven, and I knew Miti had put it in there knowing we'd be home while this new girl was being shown the apartment. Miti knew me too well, especially how to calm the wolf. After all, she was a wolf herself, even if she hardly shifted these days.

"Boss, your blood pressure! Remember what the doctor said," Damon cautioned.

"Screw my doctor! Again, why *that* apartment?" I put my head in my hands and let it drop to the counter. If I didn't know how much my grandmother loved me, I'd think she was spying on me for my father. But I knew I was in safe hands with Miti, even if she was meddlesome. "Curse Brandon to the three moons! He knew Miti wouldn't be able to resist helping her."

"Miti has a mind of her own. She doesn't need persuasion," Damon said.

"It wasn't persuasion," I growled. "The girl reeked of fear.

She's running from something, and Miti can't say no to that. She has to save every lost soul that comes her way."

"But that's what we love about her," Brent said, pulling out dishes in preparation for the lasagna.

I slammed my hand on the counter in frustration. "She knew I didn't want anyone living in that unit for a long while, especially a girl."

"Who's sexy too," Damon added, giving Brent a high five.

Jealousy shot through me. It came so suddenly that it took me by surprise.

"Boss, if you aren't interested in the new girl, can we have some fun with her?" Damon then asked.

This time my response shocked me. "No!" I growled. "You are never to go near her! Do you hear me? No one is to touch her."

They both retreated. "Of course, boss," Damon murmured, head bowed.

"Just don't bother her," I said in a more even tone. Anger management was not my strong suit. I'd been seeing a therapist, but only because Miti set it up and wouldn't take no for an answer.

They both busied themselves in the kitchen, saved by the ding of the timer denoting the lasagna was done. But I wasn't hungry. "I need to go out for a bit. Don't eat all the lasagna."

Without waiting for their response, I escaped out into the hallway, taking a deep breath when the door closed. My thoughts battled with each other. My wolf wanted to find this new girl and hunt her down, but I forced myself to the elevator and pressed the call button. All I needed was to go on a walk. That's all I needed. My head would clear and—

"Hi."

I turned to see her standing right behind me, head cocked to one side and eyes looking at me with expectation. I was a goner! I was so deep in my thoughts I didn't even smell her approach.

"Are you going to go in?" she asked, gesturing behind me.

"What?"

"The elevator," she said, now pointing to the open door.

A low growl came from my chest, and I instantly wished it hadn't, because I saw her jump back before she collected herself and walked around me to enter the elevator.

"Are you coming?" she now asked, her back pressed against the far wall. But for all her bravado I could hear a faint tremor in her voice.

Her smell was intoxicating. All I wanted to do was to slam her up against the wall and kiss her like there was no tomorrow. *What is wrong with me?* Releasing a breath, I told myself to pull it together and walked into the elevator. I stared at the wall, willing myself to just breathe.

"I forgot to introduce myself earlier," she continued, not phased by my awkward silence. "I'm Jill. You're Luc, right?"

I grunted, still unable to find my voice. Which made her flinch again.

She recovered by smoothing her hair back and giving me a faint smile. "Glad I remembered correctly; I'm bad with names, but I remember instructions well. I'm taking Miti's advice and going to grab some earplugs. Heard there was some howling around here at night and other noises. I'm not too worried, but she made a point about it, so I thought I'd get some just in case. So, how long have you lived here?"

Her rambling was kind of cute. My wolf was purring inside at the sound of her voice, and I was clenching my hands to keep myself from touching her. Since the grunt had made things worse, I decided speaking this time. "About two years," I said shortly.

"Oh, that's just around the time when you would start getting used to a place or start moving on."

"Yeah," I said, just to say something. I had no idea what she was talking about. This elevator ride was the longest I'd ever been on. We might as well have lived on the hundredth floor instead of the fourth.

Thankfully the doors opened to the first floor right then, and I walked out as fast as I could. The walk was going to clear my head. It was also going to get her out of my mind. *Yes, everything would be clearer after my walk.*

"Nice to meet you," I heard her say from behind, but I didn't turn back. I couldn't. I had to stay focused on the walk.

Instead of clearing my head, thoughts from my past started drifting into my mind the more I walked, including the many conversations I'd had with Miti about how I had closed myself off from the world and how she was worried about me. A wolf chose a mate for life; there would be no other lovers in our lives. But mine had betrayed me. At first, it took all I could to not run after the woman who had left me, to not chase her down and force her back home with me. But Kit had made it abundantly clear that she had no interest in returning.

I could still see the sneer on Kit's face as she walked away, hand in hand with her new beau, an alpha from another pack. It was the last time I'd seen her. The image slashed through my heart again, and I nearly collapsed right there. She'd crushed me.

As alpha of my own pack, I was expected to find a mate, a female alpha to claim as my own. Because once I'd claimed one, so could the rest of my packmates. It would be amazing to have cubs running around; evidence that we could continue our line.

My mind wandered back to the new girl, and I mulled over why I felt so strongly about her. Was it possible what I thought was love with Kit really wasn't? My wolf was nodding his head so hard I thought I'd topple over. No, it couldn't be. Jill wasn't a shifter; I could tell that much. Her eyes had gone wide upon seeing us . . . but I'd also seen a craving in them. She wanted me.

I shook my head. My reaction was lust; that was all it was. She was clearly beautiful and so petite that I could imagine her entwined in my arms with her head on my chest. *Stop it!* This wasn't going to happen. She was a neighbor, a cute one, but that was it.

I groaned in frustration. The walk was doing me no good. My mind was muddier than before I began.

JILL

"You should come out with me on Halloween night," Becca said through the phone.

She had called to see how I was doing after spending a week in my new apartment. It was so good to hear from her. "Oh, that actually sounds fun!"

"Of course, it is! You haven't been able to go out and let loose in years. We'll come up with a great costume for you, and what's even better, your ex won't be there."

A spike of dread went up my spine at the mention of Rich, and I froze. Becca continued unawares, "We're going to have fun, just like old times."

"Yeah . . . ."

Becca must have heard my hesitancy because she paused, then said, "We'll take it slow, okay, Jill? I know it's been a while, and you're not the same person you used to be, but you've been on your own for a week now and everything is going well. You love your job at the florist, and Ray said she saw you smile this morning. You're making so much progress—we should celebrate that!"

"It's okay, I think it'll be great fun, Becca. I look forward to going." I knew she'd never get off my case if I didn't agree to go to the party, and part of me did want to go, as I'd loved going to parties before I met Rich. However, the irrational part of me was saying not to go to the party, because a party was where I met Rich. It was also saying I should be smart and stay away from parties altogether, that way I'd never get in trouble again. *I should say no; that would be the smart thing to do.* I pressed my lips together, trying to prevent the words from escaping.

But Becca, being the amazing friend she was, and someone who knew me well, must have known my internal turmoil.

"Jill, I know your mind is going down in a spiral," Becca began. "I know it's because you're overthinking this. It's just a party, Jill. We'll get dressed up, go to the party, dance, hang out with others, and just have a good time. He won't be there. It'll just be you and me and a bunch of new people we will meet."

"I know, Becca." My voice was quiet but it was firm.

"Okay, then that's great! I'm so happy to hear that, Jill. This is going to be so fun! And when I come into town tomorrow, we're going shopping." There was a moment where it sounded like she pulled the phone away from her ear. She came back on a moment later. "Brandon just came by to tell me I have to go into a meeting. I'll pick you up tomorrow at ten, okay?"

"Okay."

"It's going to be fun, okay?"

I laughed. "Yes, Becca. It's going to be okay." I hung up and shook my head. Her worry was endearing, and not for the first time I thought about how lucky I was to have her in my life.

It's going to be okay, I repeated to myself, determined to banish old ghosts from the past.

The biggest and funniest costume I had seen in a long time was shoved into my arms. "Okay, I think this is the one," Becca announced excitedly. "Let's go try them on."

"Really? This is what you want to be for Halloween?"

"Why not? It's a tribute to our younger years when we sat in front of the computer and played without a worry in sight."

"That's very philosophical of you." I laughed, feeling light and free. I hadn't realized that coming out to shop for costumes was just what I needed at the end of a long week.

"You're not worried that you're going to lose face in front of that hunk who lives down the hallway from you, are you?" Becca teased.

"What? No!" I spluttered.

"That's what I thought," Becca said, laughing. "If he can't take you in a Super Mario outfit, then he's not worth it."

"Ha ha ha," I said, taking my costume and heading toward the changing room.

Secretly, I loved them, but I wasn't going to give in to Becca just yet. I looked at my friend, who was just putting the green hat for Luigi on her head, and said, "You sure you don't want the sexy witch or sexy police officer? That was more our style in the old days."

"I'm sure. I want us to be comfortable and just have fun tomorrow."

I knew what she meant was that she wanted *me* to be comfortable and just have fun. The reminder was like a douse of cold water, and I could feel a range of emotions start to pull me down again. My mind started spiraling with thoughts of how I was holding Becca back and ruining her life with my problems. The thoughts swam around in my mind, locking in place so that I couldn't think of anything else.

I felt a hand on my shoulder, and I looked up to see Becca looking at me, worry written all over her face. I put on a smile as best as I could, but the sight of her dressed up as Luigi soon had my smile evolve into a genuine laugh.

Becca smiled back, her relief visible. "That's better. You need to smile and laugh more." She leaned in close, placing a hand on my arm. "I'm worried about you, Jill. Have you thought more about talking to a therapist?"

I swallowed, the laughter erasing with her question. "Yeah, I'm just not ready to go yet."

"Okay, but I—"

"Let's not talk about it right now, okay?" I said with a forced smile. "Let's purchase these costumes, because I really love what you've picked out, Becca. Mario and his sidekick are going to a Halloween party!"

"That's right," Becca said, her lips hesitantly curving back into a smile to match mine. "We're going to be the stars of the party."

I laughed at her statement. I'm pretty sure we'd be far from that.

JILL

WE DONNED our costumes at my place and drove twenty minutes out of town to the community center where the party was being held. It was lit up like Christmas! Orange lights hung around every edge of the building, including the entranceway, which looked like the open jaw of a monster with paper mache fangs welcoming you into its belly. Techno beats were drifting out the doorway, and I could feel my feet starting to tap to the beat as we stood in line waiting to have our invitations scanned. There were all sorts of costumes here tonight, ranging from hockey players, to wolves, to a bee costume, and even to her partner, the farmer.

A group of five men were standing off to the side, all wearing the same costume, which included a black t-shirt and black jeans, and each of them had a wolf mask covering their whole head. They looked like bodyguards the way they were standing, and sure enough, right then, one of the masked men escorted a male dressed in only his pants out the door. The half-naked male was exclaiming a bunch of profanity, and when he tried to head back into the party, a couple of the other wolf men came to stand in front of him. The half-dressed man didn't even stand a chance when he tried to swing a punch at the masked men. Before I could blink, he was knocked to the ground with a bleeding nose.

I froze when I saw the blood spurting from his nose, rich and red and flowing freely. The sight of it triggered memories of Rich and the many times he'd beaten up others to get what he wanted. I could feel vomit start to surge up my throat. I ran to the woods, far away from the crowd, with Becca following close behind.

"You okay, Jill?" I felt her hands pulling my hair back, which had come out of Mario's hat.

I couldn't talk as bile was purged from my stomach. Tears were streaming down my face. "I can't do this, Becca. I need to go home," I managed to rasp between heaves.

"Okay, let me just tell Brandon we're heading out, and I'll take you home."

"Brandon is here?" I tried to turn to look at Becca, but my head spun.

"Yeah, he and his brothers put this party on every year. He thought it would be a safe place for you to wet your feet."

I groaned, slowly pushing upright. "I want to stay then."

"It's okay, Jill. I can take you home."

"No, I want to stay," I insisted. Brandon and Becca were the reason I was free now. If he thought this was a safe place to wet my feet, I wouldn't bail on him now.

"Why don't I ask if there's a private place for us to sit inside?" Becca rubbed a hand up and down my back, and I started to calm down.

"Is everything okay?" a deep voice suddenly said from behind us.

We both turned to see who it was, but the man had a wolf mask on, and we were so far away from the light outside the club that I couldn't discern his features.

"Everything's fine," Becca said. "We just needed a moment."

I couldn't say anything because something about his presence was familiar. A longing came over me, along with a sudden urge to raise my hand to take off his mask or touch his arms—anything to be closer to him. That's when I noticed he had a cup of water in his hands, which he was holding out to me.

"I thought you might like some water to clear your palate," he said.

It was at that point I wished I had a mask on, because I could feel a blush starting to sweep across my cheeks. I couldn't decide if it was from embarrassment due to the vomit he could no doubt smell, or the warm feelings I was having for him, but I was hyper-aware of the people lined up out front the club who were starting to stare at us.

I took the glass from his hand to move things along. "Thanks. That's very kind of you."

"Why don't you come in? I have something that might help you."

"Okay," I replied, though I had no idea why I said that. I didn't even know the guy!

The crowd parted, and we followed Mr. Wolf—as I decided to call him—through the jaws of the doorway and into the rhythmic beat of thrashing bodies. There were a lot of people crammed inside, and I could smell sweat emanating from the dancers.

I instantly grabbed Becca's hand and kept close to Mr. Wolf. Rich would have fit right in here . . . .

Wait! A few months before I left him, Rich had started calling his group 'Wolfhound.' *What if this was his group?* The men all had masks on, and their bodies were all cut just like Rich's group. Could it really be them?

I could feel my heart rate increase, and I squeezed Becca's

hand tighter, giving her a frantic look. The dancers moved in, starting to surround me. Their hands and arms and bodies started to blur together, and I could feel my legs slowly giving out. *This was a bad idea. I'm not ready for this.* The last thing I felt were strong arms closing around me. I heard Becca's shout before it all went black.

I woke up on something soft, with my face lying against a fleece-like material. A groan escaped my mouth, and I rolled over and opened my eyes to see an office desk and a number of bookshelves with hoards of books. Becca was walking toward me from the office chair. I tried to sit up, but she held me down, and I saw the look of worry in her eyes. Why worry about aging when you could have a friend like me that could expedite your life expectancy? I owed her another apology.

"I'm sorry, Becca."

"Don't be sorry, sweetheart. You're going through a lot, and I pushed you too hard too soon. I shouldn't have asked you to come to this party. I should be the one who's sorry."

"Don't say that!" I groaned again. I could really use some Advil right about now.

As if hearing my thoughts, Becca reached over and picked up a glass of water and two pills. "Here, Luc left you some Advil and a Tums for when you woke up."

"Luc?" I sat up so fast my stomach did a little lurch. I fell back into Becca's lap with my hand over my head.

"Yeah, he's been so sweet. You should have seen him. He caught you before you hit the floor and brought you straight up here. I think this is his private office. Here, take this; you look like you need it."

"I do, thanks." I chugged back the Advil and gave her back

the glass. "I've made such an idiot of myself in front of my new neighbor."

Becca shook his head. "No, you didn't. Luc's actually really concerned. He's come by no less than six times in the last thirty minutes to check on you."

"Really?" I could feel another blush stain my cheeks at the thought of him being so attentive. Then a thought dawned on me. "Was he the one who was in the wolf mask escorting us in?"

"Yeah. He's Brandon's older brother."

"Oh!"

"Yeah, I was surprised too. Brandon doesn't like talking about his family, though I can tell he loves them." Becca looked sad for a moment, then she gave me a sheepish smile as she wiped her eyes. "This room must be really dusty; I keep tearing up."

I just smiled and said, "Well, I think I should go say thanks, and then I'd like to head home."

"Okay. I'm sorry for pushing you, Jill. I'm just so happy you're okay."

I looked at Becca and saw tears forming again in the corner of her eyes. "Oh, Becca, don't be sorry. You're the one who got me out of my tight spot in the first place. You're the best friend a girl could have." I sat up to give her a tight hug. "Look, if you'll go make the request to have them play our song, I'll do a quick dance with you before we head out. We'll call it my first dance in a new world."

She laughed, and a smile crossed my lips in return. After ruining her night, it was the least I could do to let her have a little fun before I dragged us out.

"You're up," announced a familiar voice.

I turned to see Luc standing at the door with his mask off, a concerned look on his face. A part of me wanted him to come over and wrap me in his arms, but I pushed that thought quickly out of my mind. It was ludicrous. We didn't even know each other.

I gave him a small smile. "Yeah, I am. Becca told me what you did for me. Thank you."

"It was nothing. How are you feeling?" He walked over and leaned on the edge of his office desk.

"I'm doing much better. I was just telling Becca that if she could request our song, we'd dance a number before heading out."

"You should stay," he said in that deep voice that resonated inside me.

We stared at each other for what seemed like an eternity, and I couldn't help thinking that I wanted to stay . . . with him.

Becca broke the moment by asking, "Would your band be able to play YMCA?"

The shock that came over Luc's face almost made me convulse into laughter. It was an odd request, and I couldn't remember the last time we'd went to a party where YMCA was played. But this was Becca's and my song. It always made people laugh or scoff, and we loved it. We used to belt it out and dance all around her room when we were kids. Rich hated it and had refused to let me listen to it, which meant it was the one thing I knew that could make everything right again about tonight. Playing that song would erase all the memories that had tipped me over the edge.

Much to his credit, Luc nodded. "Yes, I think we can play that song." He tried to hide it, but I saw a small smile inching up at the corner of his mouth. He left us to go and relay the message to the band while Becca and I reconfigured our costumes in anticipation for our song.

Luc

YMCA? That was the song she wanted to dance to? It was at odds with her reaction earlier. I'd heard her heart rate spike when she was standing in line to enter, and after watching her run off into the woods and vomit, then catching her faint in the club soon after had played havoc with my emotions. I felt like I had already competed in a marathon tonight, and the party had only just started. The question that kept replaying in my mind was what could have possibly made her react in those ways?

Damon said she had been looking at them before she ran off into the woods. Just the fact she moved away from the lit building made me queasy.

It had been torture trying to keep away from her all week. It was a small town, and I had wanted to extend an invitation to her to attend the party, but I couldn't seem to get myself to ask. That would have meant having to stand close to her again, and as much as my wolf wanted me to, I couldn't do it.

Thank goodness Brandon came to the rescue. Brandon could read me like no one else could. He was a year younger than me and had a thing for Becca. Why he didn't do anything about it was anyone's guess, but he kept close to her at all times, regardless. When he finally found out I wanted to ask Jill to the party, he said he'd ask Becca and Jill on my behalf. The relief that had washed over me was embarrassing. I didn't even know Jill, yet the draw to be with her was so deep I'd been having trouble sleeping.

When Brandon reported back that the two girls were coming to our Halloween party, I'd tried to hide the burst of happiness the news brought, but he saw right through me. He warned me to keep my feelings on the down-low in case this was just a temporary infatuation, but he had no idea what I was experiencing. Brandon didn't know the way my skin tingled when I heard Jill walking by my door every day, or how it was all I could do to not follow her everywhere she went to make sure she was safe. He also didn't know I was on edge the whole time she was away and could only calm down when I heard her door click shut at the end of the day, knowing she was once again safe in the building with my pack guarding her.

JILL

WE HEARD the song come on just as we finished fixing up our costumes. Both of us squealed and ran out of the room, down the stairs, and into the crowd. Everyone was laughing and looking at each other like they had walked into the wrong party, but Becca and I knew how to take care of the situation.

"Let's go!" I cried out to her.

We both ran into the middle of the crowd and started jumping up and down. I wouldn't say I knew how to dance but my body remembered how to have fun, especially to YMCA. Within a couple of minutes, a few more people joined us, and then a few more after that. About mid-way through the song the whole place was jumping up and down. It was fantastic. I let my inhibitions drift away for those five minutes and enjoyed the happy vibes that surged through me.

At one point I glanced toward the bar and saw Luc staring at me. I shot him a smile and waved at him to join us, but he didn't budge. I shrugged and continued dancing.

When the music ended, I was sweating. I also felt the biggest smile on my face that I hadn't exhibited in years. *Maybe it wouldn't be so bad if I stayed for just another song?*

Becca interrupted my thoughts when she put a hand on my shoulder. "Jill, I want you to meet someone."

I turned to see a very attractive man standing next to Becca. Tall and strong like Luc but not as intimidating. He exuded a relaxed air about him. The other thing I noticed was that he seemed unable to take his eyes off Becca, and his hand was slowly inching across her waist.

"Jill, this is Brandon," Becca announced. "Brandon, this is my friend, Jill."

"Oh my goodness!" I flung my arms around him and gave him a big hug.

A rumbling laugh emanated from deep within his chest. He hugged me back for a second before stepping back and extending his arm. "Hi, Jill. It's great to finally meet you. You are looking well."

I shook his hand and wondered why the formality when I felt, more than saw, someone walk up behind me. I turned to see Luc looking at Brandon and Becca. He was standing a bit close, but I somehow felt safer with him right behind me instead of intimidated. Brandon, on the other hand, seemed to have an amused look on his face.

"You two have never met before?" Luc asked Brandon, now looking between us.

How could he have heard us talking while standing over by the bar and with the music so loud?

"No, we haven't," Brandon said. I stiffened, thinking Brandon was going to tell Luc about my ex, but Brandon was clearly a gentleman as well as a good lawyer and didn't say anything about that. "Becca needed help with some research, and I provided my expertise. That was all. There was no reason to meet face to face."

I gave Becca a side look and saw that she couldn't stop looking at Brandon. A light bulb went off in my head, and I kicked myself for being so slow at catching on. Brandon must be the guy she had a crush on, and by the way he was looking at her, the feeling was mutual. If he was the one she'd fallen for, he had better be good enough for her, because I was never going to let anyone hurt Becca.

"Let's get you home," Becca said, but I could hear the regret in her voice, and Brandon still hadn't let go of her waist.

"Why don't I take you home?" Luc suddenly announced. "I'm free."

I grabbed the lifeline he offered, wanting nothing more than to make sure Becca had a good time—and a chance to see if what was between her and Brandon led anywhere. "Yes, please! After all, you know where I live," I said to Luc with a big smile. Turning back to my friend, I said brightly, "Becca, you stay and have fun."

"You sure?" she asked, her face now pinched with worry.

"Of course, I'm sure!" I said firmly and went to give her a hug. We held each other for a bit while the two men looked on.

"Thank you for dragging me out here. I had fun in the end," I said to her quietly as I pulled away. I meant it. The dance and its associated happiness had jumpstarted something inside me, and I didn't want to let it go. I hadn't felt this happy in a very long time.

She smiled. "I'm so glad you came, but I'm also sorry for bringing you here and triggering all those memories."

"Don't be sorry! Dancing to YMCA more than made up for it. Enjoy your time tonight, Becca. I want to hear all about it later on."

"You too," she said, leaning in close again to give me another hug. "And don't go straight home. See if he wants to take you for ice cream or something," she whispered into my ear.

"Becca!"

"What?" she shot back. "He's cute, and I know you like him." She pulled back with a smirk.

"Okay, well I'm leaving," I said, turning away from her quickly. "Luc, let's go." I started heading toward the door.

But Becca grabbed me from behind and whispered in my ear, "Just think about it."

She flitted away to dance with Brandon, and I found Luc looking down at me with a question in his eyes. Did he hear what Becca said? Hmm, it was best to keep moving and play ignorant.

The crowd was so packed I had a hard time pushing through. Luc noticed and got in front of me, creating an opening with his body, and I followed behind him all the way to the entrance.

Once outside, the night air was refreshing. I closed my eyes and took in a deep breath. Maybe party scenes were behind me . . . or maybe I just needed to go home and sleep. I felt Luc's warmth as he came to stand beside me, and I let myself enjoy his scent for a second before opening my eyes.

I gave a short gasp at the sight of him. His eyes were piercing and staring right into mine, filled with longing. He seemed tense, as if he wanted something he couldn't get. My eyes went down to his chest, where I could see his shirt moving up and down with each breath. It was all I could do to not reach out and touch him.

"Shall we go?" he rasped, breaking the taut silence.

"Yes, let's." *Anything to take my mind off whatever is going on here.*

I followed him to his car, where he opened the door for me to get in. This small gesture wasn't lost on me, because I couldn't remember the last time anyone had opened a door for me and actually meant it. Rich only did it when we were in public, and only when he was talking with someone else, so the gesture meant nothing.

We drove in silence for a bit. The whole time I was aware of how close Luc was to me. I watched his hands grip the steering wheel. The knuckles were white, as if he needed to hold onto something or he'd fall apart.

I dared to turn my head and peek at his profile. My first thought was how long his eyelashes were. So not fair. But my eyes quickly moved down to his nose and then his lips, which were pinched together as tight as his fingers.

"What are you looking at?" he asked teasingly.

I snapped my face back to looking straight ahead, feeling a sudden onrush of blood to my cheeks and neck. I heard a chuckle and snapped back to face Luc again, then felt a sharp twinge in my neck. "Ow!"

Before I could reach up to rub it, his hand was on the spot, massaging it loose. I almost melted into a puddle. His hands felt rough but warm, and even with all his muscles, his touch was gentle as it worked around my neck, loosening the knot before it got worse.

"Got to be careful there when you're looking," he said, chuckling again.

"I wasn't looking." A big fat lie, and we both knew it. To his credit, he didn't laugh again.

His hand left my neck, and I swallowed a sigh. Why couldn't he have left his hand there a little longer?

"Feeling better?" he asked softly.

"Yeah, thanks."

We got to the first traffic light, and I realized I didn't want to go home and be done with the night. Ice cream might not be a bad idea. I cleared my throat. "Luc?"

"Yeah?"

I just had to say it. It was no big deal. He was just my neighbor and we were stopping for a snack on the way home. "Would you like to have some ice cream before dropping me off?"

I held my breath while I waited on his response, ready to start putting my walls up again if he denied me, but he responded, "I'd love to. I know just the place."

The smile that broke across his face was tantalizing. I could have stared at him forever.

A few blocks away, we stopped at Mama's Homemade Ice Cream. This was my kind of place!

I got out of the car and was already walking toward the window before Luc could come around to open my door. They had a huge whiteboard nailed to the side of the building that listed close to a hundred different flavors. Oh, they had soft-serve too! I felt like I had died and gone to heaven.

"I've never seen anyone so happy to see ice cream," Luc said.

I turned to see him standing only a foot away. My breath caught at the smell of him. He smelt fresh, like the woods and the clean air of this town. "Well, you've never met me," I said with a smile.

"That's true," he said. "But I'm glad I have."

Thank goodness we were next in line because I could feel my cheeks warming up. I ordered a chocolate peanut butter scoop on a waffle cone and smothered it in fudge for good measure, while Luc ordered a banana split sundae with three scoops of ice cream, a mountain of whipped cream, and a cherry on top.

"You're going to eat all that?" I gasped.

"I missed dinner tonight with planning the party and all."

I nodded. "Okay, that makes sense."

But I couldn't help thinking if he ate like that, how did he keep such a sexy physique? *Oh right, he actually exercises, while you've been locked away in your own home for two years.* The pain of having to deal with what I'd suffered at the hands of Rich overwhelmed my senses for a moment. It wasn't for long, but it was long enough that Luc noticed something was amiss.

To my surprise, he took my hand. "Do you want to talk about it?"

He wanted to know my thoughts? He was too perfect. I had thought the same about Rich when I first met him, but Luc felt different. He was quiet and didn't push, very unlike the loud, boisterous person Rich was. It probably wasn't fair to compare Luc with Rich, either. The likelihood of Luc being in a gang did not seem likely.

I mulled over his question. Was there a reason to keep my past a secret? It was not like Rich and I were splattered on tabloids. I decided then and there that Luc would be the first one I would share my past with.

"Everything just reminds me of my ex," I said quietly.

I saw him tense, and now that I had said the words out loud, I regretted saying anything. Maybe I should take Becca up on finding that therapist. Pushing the thought aside, I said, "Sorry, I haven't really socialized in quite a while. We don't need to talk about my past. It's boring, anyways."

"I doubt it's boring," he replied swiftly. "So, does that mean you're not seeing anyone right now?"

"Yeah, I'm free. Finally."

"Finally?" he probed.

Ugh, another slip. I almost face-palmed my forehead. "My ex was very controlling," I explained. "It wasn't . . . the best of relationships."

"I see." His hands went to his hair, and he looked distraught. That was my doing, and I felt horrible.

I had to get ahold of my emotions. This wasn't going to do if people around me could pick up on my distress. Even Ray had asked me the other day if I was okay when I saw a bouquet of lilies. The flowers had started to make me cry because Rich used to give me those when we had just started dating. Of course, the lilies became nonexistent once I'd moved in with him, just like all the romance.

41

I finally looked at Luc and realized he had already eaten half of his sundae. "Wow, you must have been starving."

He gave me a sheepish grin. "This is one of my favorite places. I love ice cream."

"I do too. It's my favorite dessert."

He smiled at me, and I could have sworn his eyes were probing. I didn't want to dim the mood further by sharing more about myself, but Luc thought otherwise.

"Did you date him long?" he now asked.

I swallowed a scoop of ice cream to regain my confidence. "Almost three years. Long enough."

"You seem relieved and not sad about leaving him."

"Why would you say that?"

"Your forehead creases when you're sad, but when you're talking about your ex, you seem more relaxed. Sad is just normally what people feel when they break up. I'm guessing it was a while ago then?"

"Just a couple weeks ago, actually."

He looked up at me with a scoop of ice cream mid-way to his mouth. "The day I first met you," he breathed.

"Well, technically, that was the day after."

"So you're fresh out of a breakup?" A jolt of pain flashed across his face. It made my heart twist, and I wanted to hold him.

"I am, but I wouldn't call it a healthy relationship. I'm not looking to go into a new one if you're asking."

"No."

Okay, he didn't have to answer that fast.

As I scrambled for a reply, he continued, "No, I mean, I wasn't asking. I didn't mean to put you on the spot. I just . . ." He trailed off and shrugged.

He looked adorable when flustered. I couldn't help but smile, to which he seemed to relax and asked, "So how's your ice cream?"

"It's delicious, thank you. This was just what I needed."

That put a smile on his face, and I was glad to see it. We talked for the remainder of our time there. I learned that his father owned the apartment complex, but he was working on a way to buy it from him. Luc wanted to be an entrepreneur and invest in real estate—at least, that's what he was thinking of doing right now as he had a tendency to jump around on ideas and his father was getting frustrated with him. There were a lot of issues with his father I was gathering, and I could relate. Having not had a father figure, a therapist would probably say that's why I ended up with Rich, but I didn't want to share that with Luc. It's not like we were going out, this was just ice cream. Besides, I had already caused enough turmoil already, and it was nice to have a new friend.

A new friend. That put a smile on my face.

"What are you smiling about?"

"You're my first friend I've made in a while. That's enough to put a smile on my face," I said, feeling contentment roll over me. Now that was a feeling I was not used to.

"You have a beautiful smile."

"Thanks," I said, feeling a blush coming on strong as he studied me. I balled up my napkin and looked at his finished sundae. "Well, that's the last of the ice cream. Shall we head home?" I ducked my head and bent down for my bag before he saw my whole face and neck turn red.

"Yeah, lets." He got up without another look back, and I hurried to catch up with him.

When we got back to the apartment, he walked me to the door. We lingered there for a moment, and I contemplated what had happened tonight. "I had a fun night," I ended up saying.

"I did too. You going to be okay?" He didn't seem to want to leave, and if I could admit it to myself, I didn't really want him to either.

Before I could start leaning toward him, I made myself say, "Yes, I'll be fine. I'll see you later. Thanks for the ride home." I then quickly unlocked my door, went inside, and shut the door without looking back.

I kept my hand on the door, listening for his footsteps to walk toward his place, but no sound came. Instead, I heard a sigh that sounded like it had come from deep within; a sigh that carried a lot of baggage. I so wanted to go back out into the hallway and ask him what was wrong, but instead, I just stood there.

At the sound of his footsteps retreating, I leaned against the door and slid to the floor. My heart was pounding so fast. What had just happened? This was crazy. I didn't even know Luc. We had shared a little about ourselves, but nothing more than new friends would, and yet I felt strongly for Luc, more than I had ever felt for Rich. It told me this wasn't lust but something more.

Oh no, I *was* going crazy! Who would want to jump into a relationship right after getting out of a horrid one? I needed alone time. And maybe tomorrow I'd call Becca to help me find a therapist. Yeah, that sounded like the perfect plan. She could talk me out of my ridiculous thoughts.

LUC

THIS WAS NOT GOING to work. Not at all. I was falling for her more than I cared to admit. I needed to run, and run I did. I threw caution to the wind and shifted before I hit the tree line. The more I ran, the more my thoughts drew away from how good Jill smelled, how soft her skin looked, and how her heart pounded when she was near me.

Why did she stay behind that door waiting for me to leave? Her breathing had gotten fast, and I'd had to peel myself away from her door to get away. Why was this happening? I was never this bad when I was with Kit. She never drove my wolf crazy like this. All I wanted to do was wrap Jill up in my arms and never let her go. Be her savior in everything. Never let anyone hurt her again. Whoever this slimeball ex-boyfriend was better be sure to never cross my path.

After Kit, I had promised myself to never let another girl in. They were too fickle. One look from another guy and they were off, not caring that my heart was shattering. *Jill will be the same,* I told myself. *You should move on while you have the chance.*

I loved the feel of the wind blowing through my fur while

I ran through the woods. This was where I belonged, and it was a huge part of who I was. Jill wasn't part of this world or of the pack, and there was no need to ever bring her in on it. I realized then that if I was going to get through this infatuation with Jill, then I had to make *her* stay away from me. I pondered on how I could do that as I ran. The thought hit me almost immediately—my brothers hadn't come to visit in a while, and this gave me the perfect opportunity to invite them over. They'd each bring a couple of their pack members, and maybe the sight of us all together would intimidate Jill enough that she'd become scared and leave. I didn't know what had brought her to our town, but I couldn't allow her to stay.

I stopped running and breathed in the cool air. Yes, that would be exactly what I'd do. I'd call them tomorrow and set up a time to come visit me soon. And the sooner the better; my wolf couldn't take this much longer.

JILL

"So, what happened?" Becca asked over a platter of freshly-made waffles with real maple syrup drizzled over them.

She had woken me up the next morning with a solid pounding at the door. Good thing for her I was already awake. Last night was filled with tossing and turning; I'd been tormented by constant images of Luc, with his sultry eyes staring back at me as he leaned toward my wanting lips.

"Hello to Jill! Yoohoo!"

"Huh? What?" I blinked at Becca.

"You're daydreaming about Luc, aren't you?"

"No, I'm not," I said, but even I could tell I'd said that maybe a bit too quickly.

Becca was looking at me with a knowing look. "You just keep telling yourself that."

I didn't dare respond, but she persisted. "Come on, tell me. Did he drop you off at home, or did y'all go someplace else? Please tell me you didn't come straight home."

"I didn't," I said, and I could feel a blush coming on. "But it's not what you think."

"You did go for ice cream!"

"Okay, fine, it is what you think."

She got out of her chair and came over, pulling me into a huge hug. "I'm so happy for you."

"We didn't do anything," I said against her shoulder.

She pulled back and gripped my shoulders. "But it's still a big step for you, Jill! You were eating ice cream with someone you just met, and you enjoyed it."

"How do you know I enjoyed it?"

"Because your skin has turned a nice shade of pink," she said, smiling.

Drats. This was what got me in trouble with Rich. He could read me like an open book because I couldn't hide my feelings. Well, I was going to do better with Luc. I could stand my ground.

In order to change the subject, I decided now was a good time to ask Becca about a therapist. "So, I wanted to tell you that I think I'm ready to talk to a therapist."

"Really?" Becca was looking at me with big eyes, and I couldn't help but laugh—another thing I had missed doing in the last two years. It felt good to laugh again.

"Yes," I said firmly. I was going to do this. I needed to get my life back together again, and I was sure the therapist would tell me to stay away from Luc. It was what I needed—someone on the outside telling me to stay away from him for my own good.

Becca clapped her hands. "Great! I have just the person. She already has you down for Mondays at one in the afternoon, so I'll take you there tomorrow."

"What?" Now it was my turn to look at her with big eyes.

"I was going to drag you to see her even if you didn't want to. She's a good friend of mine. I trust her, and I think you'll like her too."

I gave her the stink eye but couldn't help but feel loved that Becca was still looking out for me.

She continued, "Because you made me such a yummy breakfast, I'm going to let you in on a little secret."

"Oh?"

She looked down for a moment and ran her tongue over her lips, then said slowly, "Brandon—"

"Oh! How was your night?" This time I gave *her* a knowing look, but Becca waived my question away.

"We're just coworkers who have fun together, Jill. He's like a friendly plus-one, and in return, I'm his plus one when he needs one. And if you must know, we danced the night away and then he took me home. That was it, nothing special."

I eyed her. "That's it? What about that guy you told me you had a crush on?"

"It's not Brandon," Becca said quickly.

"You could have fooled me with the way you two were looking at each other last night."

Becca turned a nice shade of pink at this, and I knew I had hit the mark. Why was she denying it?

"There's nothing going on," she insisted.

Clearly, she was not ready to admit it. "Lame. You two should go on a real date sometime."

"Why? Neither one of us wants to get tied down." This comment came out with such venom I knew there was more to this story than she was letting on.

"Hey, I'm not going to dig, you two just look so sweet together."

"Yeah, that's what people say." Her anger deflated, and she forced a smile back on her face. "Now, before you so rudely interrupted me, as I was saying, Brandon knows of another party in a few weeks that we can go to. He was able to get us in, and I'm taking you with me. Last night didn't start off great, but I think it really helped you open up a little bit."

I began to shake my head. "Becca, I don't think that's a

good idea. It's too much too soon. Look at how I reacted last night."

"Last night *was* too much too soon, but the next party isn't until a few weeks from now. You'll have plenty of time to continue to get used to your new life. You'll be coming with me again, and I'll look after you. Besides, did I mention it's going to be a masquerade party?"

"What?" I squealed.

"Thought you might like that," she said, smiling. "Especially because we've always said we'd go to a masquerade ball together, and this will be just like the ones we read in stories! We have to go, Jill. I'm not going to let you wallow in your apartment by yourself when there's life to be lived outside these four walls."

"But I'm not that same person anymore, Becca."

"Then attend the party for me! Come on, you can't say no; Brandon already got us tickets."

"It's just the three of us, then?"

"Well, no. Luc is also coming." Becca held up a hand when she saw my startled look. "Brandon will be asking him today, so we'll see."

"Becca!"

"But you just admitted you had fun last night when you went for ice cream with Luc."

"Yeah, but the ball is different. This would be like going on a date. Last night was just a friend helping out a friend."

"Oh, pish posh! I think it was the same thing, and you know it. Albeit, it was a very short date, but it was still a date."

"No, it wasn't," I said under my breath, and I crossed my arms over my chest. How was I going to get out of this?

The next two weeks flew by. I worked at the florist during the day and saw Robin for therapy sessions at night. Unfortunately for me, Robin was excited about Luc. She said it might be a safe way to meet a new guy friend and that I shouldn't discount the possibility of it becoming more. He wasn't Rich, she said. But Rich wasn't someone I could just get over. He had been a gentleman at the beginning, just like Luc was.

Thankfully, Becca didn't bring up going to the masquerade ball again. She knew I didn't own another costume, and she made no mention of going out to get one, so I relaxed into my day-to-day routine and enjoyed the freedom of living my life the way I wanted.

I had started taking a walk through the woods on my lunch break. There was a calming stream about five hundred yards in. A log that looked as though it had fallen down years ago made the perfect seat for me to rest on and take in the scene. The birds chirping and twittering added a nice ambient sound to the background, and I let myself forget about my past while I sat there. The therapist had told me to listen to the stream and let it calm me. She said I should allow thoughts of Rich and my previous life to filter through my mind and just let them go.

I had been practicing this exercise on the same log every day for two weeks, and I had calmed down so much that, at first, I didn't notice the wolf approach. I immediately jumped up and started backing away, hoping I could escape before he thought I was his next meal, but he didn't move.

The white wolf lay about ten feet away and was looking at me with dark, familiar eyes. His paws were crossed on top of each other, and his head rested on them in a calm repose. A closer look showed that he had dark markings around his ears. The markings looked familiar; I was sure I had glimpsed him between the trees during my previous visits. Was it the same wolf who had passed by on the other side of the stream yesterday? The same one who had looked at me for a few seconds before going about his business? If I didn't know any better, it was like he had come here today with a purpose, and that purpose was me—not to eat, but for company.

"You want to hear something crazy?" I asked the wolf.

Did his eyebrows just lift? I shook my head to clear the thought.

"I thought you had come to see me," I confessed. "Is that not the most ridiculous thing you've ever heard?" I sighed. "I should be trembling in front of you, but you look harmless. You're a lot bigger than I imagined a wolf to be, but you should have seen my ex. He was also a bigger than average person; he towered over people at six feet nine." I laughed and shook my head. "I can't believe I stayed with him for so long."

This time I could have sworn I saw one of his ears twitch. Sitting back down on the log, I told myself that at least the wolf was a living creature that I could talk to. When Rich would lock me up, I'd found myself talking to the plush animals I'd accumulated each time Rich came to say sorry. For some reason, he thought the plushies would alleviate my anger toward him. I couldn't have cared less about the gifts, because I was too scared to be angry, although they did provide me with some company when I was locked up. Of course, the conversation was one-way, but I could still get my worries off my chest.

"You know, when I first met my ex, I was so impressed by his talent," I continued to the wolf. "He's a plastic surgeon at the hospital in the city. A good one too. He was always being invited to parties by clients that praised his work. He took me to those parties, and I had a blast at the beginning." I turned to look at the stream as I felt a tear flow down my cheek. "It was all fun and games then, I know that now. I was so naïve."

A whine came from the wolf's direction, and I turned to see his sad eyes looking back at me.

"You understand, don't you? Did someone hurt you too? Relationships are so difficult. How do you know you're getting into the right one?"

His head was raised, and both his ears were up, as if he were trying to hear me better. I smiled at the thought that I had a captive audience.

"I'm seeing a therapist now. She said for me to think of something about my ex that I didn't hate. But it's so hard to do that, as all I can think of are the bad things these days. But there was a time when things were okay. It's taken me the whole of this week to come up with something, but I just remembered that he used to let me help him with a side project."

An ear definitely twitched toward me at this news.

"He had this makeshift lab in a back room where these wonderful and sometimes not so pleasant smells would waft out. Sometimes the house would smell like gardenias, and even when he wasn't there." I shook my head. "I'm jumping all over the place, sorry. The thing is, he always smelled like gardenias, and it was one of the things I found attractive about him." I laughed. "Now I find it repulsive. The odd thing was that sometimes the place would smell of gardenias when he wasn't home. I questioned him about it, and he showed me the lab then. He told me he had always liked science, and it was a hobby of his to experiment. I assumed he was creating perfumes, but who really knew?" I shrugged. "He never brought me into that lab again, nor did I smell that pungent, gardenia smell anymore. There was only a pleasant waft whenever he was around."

The wolf had put his head back down again and was looking at me like a child waiting for the next part of the story.

"Rich continued doing whatever he was doing in his lab. He was making this liquid that he used to bottle up. He would let me package them up for him, and the labels said how much you could drink at a certain time. I never found out who he was sending them to or what they were for, but I often wonder if his experiments had anything to do with the men who started coming by randomly."

I shook my head and looked at the wolf again. I must be going crazy if I was talking to a wolf like this. But I couldn't leave him hanging without the ending; he had been a wonderful listener. "You've been a fantastic listener," I said to him. "Maybe you could meet me here again someday? Then at least I won't be talking to myself."

The wolf, sensing I wasn't going to say anything more, got up on his legs. He really was huge. Beautiful, though, with his white coat and dark markings on his ears. I felt an urge to reach out and run my hands through his fur, but before I could act, he turned and jumped over the stream, running off into the forest without looking back.

I waved at him and smiled, hoping to see him again.

Luc

I SAT SLUMPED AGAINST A TREE, not too far from where Jill was sitting on the log but where she couldn't see me. I could still hear her heartbeat and her soft breathing. She'd talked to me, and it was devastating. Even the wetness in her eyes hadn't escaped me.

I squeezed my eyes shut, my heart aching to run back to her. My wolf was screaming in my head that I had gone in the wrong direction, leaving her all alone. I should be comforting her, not wallowing under this tree.

But I couldn't. What if she was another Kit?

The only comfort I could grasp at that moment was that my brothers, Jacob and Bruno, had both agreed to visit me on the pretense that I missed them. If they only knew . . . .

JILL

THE NEXT WEEK FLEW BY, but I didn't see the wolf again. I did talk to a bird and a squirrel at one point, but it wasn't the same; they stayed for only a few seconds before flying or running away.

By this point, I had totally forgotten about the masquerade ball and was just enjoying my mundane life. However, on the night of the ball, Becca showed up with two dress bags in her arms.

"What is this?" I asked her, a sinking feeling in my gut.

"Our costumes!" she announced, with the biggest grin on her face.

"We're really going, aren't we?"

"Of course. Did you think I forgot?"

"I was hoping so."

There was a poignant silence between us before Becca pulled me into a hug. "I'm sorry, Jill. I just want to get the old Jill back. Look, if you don't want to go tonight, it's okay."

Relief surged through me, but it faded when I saw the sadness in Becca's eyes. It reminded me that everything I had lived through had been carried by Becca. It was a miracle she was still even talking to me!

The one thing Rich had let me have was a cell phone, one that he monitored. Becca was one of the only people he'd allowed me to talk to, and only once every two weeks.

Becca hadn't even told me she was going to get me out of there. The one time she had tried to talk "business" with me on the phone, I'd gotten beaten up by Rich. From that point onward, we'd only talked about safe subjects, like what flowers she was growing in her garden, what restaurant she had visited that week, what was the latest movie she'd gone to see, and her crush—who I still thought was Brandon. We had learned to speak about anything but the subject of my freedom.

These thoughts slammed into my mind as she stood there, waiting on my response. She'd done so much for me, and this ball obviously meant a lot to her. If she wanted me to come with her to another party, who was I to say no? I owed her more than I knew. Plus, there was also the fact that I couldn't get the last party out of my mind . . . or a certain man.

"No, I'm the one that should be sorry," I now said. "You've done so much for me, Becca. And you're right, I need to get back out into the real world."

"Really?"

The surprise in her eyes almost made me cry. I had put her through so much. "Yes, really. Give me my dress. I'll go change into it right now."

She thrust the dress at me. "Okay, here. There's a mask that goes with it. You're going to love it!" she announced with a huge smile.

We got ready in record time. The dress Becca had picked out for me was stunning. It was made of black silk and was form-fitting to the waist, clinging to my chest and torso before falling into a large skirt that fanned out around my ankles when I twirled. The bodice was strapless, but ruching from the waist down added some texture, and a gold stripe lined the zipper on the back, giving it a pop of color. It was beautiful, even if it made me feel self-conscious. All I could remember was that the last time I'd shown so much skin, Rich had made me go and change. Wearing this dress would put another ghost to bed, so I swallowed my fear and stepped into it.

Becca kept up a running dialogue as we got ready, keeping us in a party mood. She did a very good job of it because, before I knew it, we had makeup on, and Becca had managed to do my hair in a low bun at the nape of my neck. Last to put on were the masks, which in themselves were exquisite. They were both gold and black with lace edging, but Becca's had a feather on one side that made it look even more beautiful.

I couldn't believe we were going to a masquerade ball! It had always been one of my dreams, and Becca knew it. She tied the ribbon on my mask and stepped around to stand in front of me. Her eyes grew wide, and she let out a loud squeal. "You look absolutely stunning, Jill! Wait till Luc sees you." I opened my mouth to brush her comment off, but Becca cut in with, "One off the bucket list, yeah?"

I gave a sigh. "You know me well." I turned to take another look in the mirror and felt a prickly sensation in my fingers as I eyed my appearance. It was hard to believe that was me staring back.

Becca knew I could never say no to a masquerade ball, not after that night we'd found her mom's mask in the back of her closet when we were teenagers. That night had been the first of many where we'd pretended to attend one. It was unreal to think we were now going to a real one! I told myself firmly that I was going to have fun tonight, no matter what happened.

"Are you ready?" Becca asked.

"I'll just be a second. You go down first."

Halfway to the door, she turned back to look at me. "You okay?"

"Yes, I'm fine!" I said with a laugh. "I just want to take one last, long look at myself in the mirror."

She smiled. "You're too funny. Okay, don't be long; I hear doors opening. That might be Luc coming to get you."

Why did she have to say that? The prickling in my fingers got worse then. I leaned against the wall of my room and breathed in and out like Robin had shown me. Everything was going to be fine. We were just going as friends. Nothing had to happen. There were no expectations. I was going to get my life back and enjoy living again; I just needed to keep repeating this to myself for the rest of the night until I made it back to my room. I sighed. Even I knew that was a ridiculous thing to think and do.

I took one more breath to slow my heartbeat down and reminded myself Becca had gone to a lot of trouble to get this invitation, not to mention the dress and mask. I needed to go down and meet her; I couldn't leave her waiting.

Somehow, I made it into the hallway, and when I turned to lock the door, I heard a few clicks behind me. I turned to see a couple of doors opening. Out stepped two men, built just as big as Luc. Where did these men come from? Behind them came a few more men, and I started to get a little nervous. I could stand up for myself, but not against these burly men. Their muscles were like rock, and there were many of them.

I hadn't seen them before and wondered if they lived here or had just moved in. I'd been so deep into my new routine I hadn't noticed. Maybe this wasn't the best place for me to live. Maybe I had settled for it too quickly and should have kept looking. But it had felt so right!

My heart started beating fast, and I suddenly froze, standing there in the hallway.

"Hi, you must be Jill," one of the men said. He held out his hand, but I couldn't move to accept it.

The second guy said, "We're Luc's brothers, Jacob and Bruno. These are our friends. We come and stay every once in a while."

So they did live here at times. But they reminded me too much of Rich's men. I could feel goosebumps arising on my arms, and I held my hands together to keep them from shaking. This wasn't going well.

At that moment I heard another door open, and Luc came walking out . . . not dressed for a masquerade ball. At least, torn jeans and what looked like a white undershirt weren't what I would qualify as masquerade ball material.

A surge of disappointment washed over me, followed by a strange mix of relief and desire, but most of all, confusion. How could one person cause me to feel so much in one instant? I felt like a fool thinking he'd come with me. What was I thinking? I started walking down the hall, ignoring the men who had just introduced themselves and trying my best not to look at Luc as I stared straight ahead at the elevator doors, willing them to open before I got there.

"You look beautiful."

His voice stopped me. I turned to look at him and almost lost my resolve. His eyes were dark as they roamed my body from head to toe. He was leaning against the doorframe, looking as if he needed it for support.

"Thanks," I said quietly.

"I can't go tonight. I have my brothers here," he said, gesturing toward the men who I knew were staring at us intensely. "Brandon told me he didn't mind escorting you on my behalf."

"I see." So I was just baggage to be bounced around for people to take care of? Okay.

"That's not what—"

"No, it's okay, I get it. Well, have a good night." I turned to leave before I said something stupid. Thank goodness the elevator doors opened then.

Another man walked out to receive greetings from the men behind me, but I didn't care. The only face I saw was Luc's as he stared back at me as the elevator doors slowly closed.

JILL

"WHAT TOOK YOU SO LONG?" Becca asked as I walked toward the car.

"Oh, you know, bumping into Luc's family and friends, all who remind me of Rich and his goons. And then there's Luc—he's not coming. Did you know that?"

"Yeah, he said he was busy," Brandon said from the other side of the car, looking annoyed. "But it's his loss. I get two beautiful women on my arms tonight."

"You sure do," Becca giggled.

I stared at her in disbelief. Becca and giggling were not two things I would have ever put together. I looked at Brandon, then back at Becca and just smiled.

We got into the car and silently drove to the ball—at least I was silent; Brandon and Becca kept up a tirade of words the entire way, which ground on my nerves. I was all dressed up to go to a ball—and not just any ball, but a masquerade ball—and I was the third wheel on my friend's date!

I thought Luc and I made a connection over ice cream. True, we hadn't really seen each other over the last few weeks, and when we did it was a slight lift of the chin in acknowledgment or a pleasant "How are you?" in the hallway, but I still thought we had made a friendly connection . . . but it seemed he thought otherwise.

Ugh! I didn't need this right now. I wanted calm days, where the only worry I had was to make beautiful bouquets for satisfied clients. I didn't need a guy to put pressure on me. Besides, Ray had dropped a hint that she had been thinking about expanding her business to the next town over, which meant I would be busy enough if that happened. I had started daydreaming about running my own floral shop. I would cater to weddings and birthdays, and any other party that needed a floral arrangement. I loved romance, but if what I'd gone through with Rich and the hot-cold scenario with Luc were anything to go by, I was happy to live vicariously through my clients.

"Earth to Jill," Becca said, sticking her head into the car. "Everything okay?"

I turned to see that we'd arrived and my door was being held open by a man in a tuxedo. Becca was looking at me with concern. I made to move out of the car, and she stood back. As soon as her head moved out of the way I saw a grand staircase that was attached to one of the largest houses I'd ever seen. The whole place was lit up. There were lights along the walkway and amongst the luscious garden surrounding the front of the house. Everywhere I looked were men in tuxedoes and women in ballgowns, all wearing masks decorated with pearls and a number of precious jewels. The fragrances on the air were ripe, and to my surprise they did not make me gag. It was beautiful.

Who cared if I was by myself? This was a dream come true! I was at an actual masquerade ball! I could feel a smile growing on my face, and when I looked back at Becca, I saw relief.

"You okay?" she asked.

"I'm good, really good. Let's go have fun," I said, hooking her arm and starting toward the stairs.

Brandon walked closely behind us. He seemed tense and was sniffing the air. Must have been my imagination, though; I didn't smell anything besides the numerous perfumes permeating from the women around me.

We blended in with the mask-wearing crowd as we lined up to get in. So, this was what it was like to have anonymity. I liked the feeling the mask gave me. I could do anything tonight, and no one would be the wiser.

We inched forward, the warm, inviting glow of the ballroom becoming more pronounced. Music wafted toward us. It almost sounded like sophisticated elevator music, soothing and gentle. I stood a little bit straighter, basking in its vibrant energy.

When it was our turn to enter, Brandon handed over our invitations, only to have one handed back. A twinge went through me as he quickly slipped it back into his shirt pocket. But Luc's absence was put to the side when I stepped through the entrance. It felt like I had walked into another world! There was the monotonous tone of many people speaking at once, and then the music overpowering them all. Servers were passing out hors d'oeuvres in tuxedos, wearing white gloves and simple black masks. It was glorious.

I gave a little squeal and squeezed Becca's arm. "We're really here, Becca!"

She squeezed me back. "I know, isn't it exciting? It's even more magical than I thought."

"I'll go grab us some drinks. What would you like?" Brandon said.

I noticed he had placed a hand on Becca's back, and I couldn't help thinking that Rich used to do that to me; gentle touches here and there.

I saw a crowd of people on the other side of the room and

decided to unhook myself as the third wheel. "Thanks, Brandon, but I'll grab one later. Why don't you two go and enjoy the party? I'm going to see what everyone is doing over there." I gestured to the area I was intending on heading.

"Okay," Becca said.

I turned to see Brandon whispering something in her ear. Yup, definitely time for me to break off and do my own thing.

I walked toward the crowd and got a couple of nods from men on the way. It made me feel good. I reminded myself I was single and dressed up in a beautiful gown, and I was going to have fun tonight.

I got closer to the crowd and saw they were looking at a display of past masquerade balls. One wall was lined with an array of masks. Some had so much detail on them that they looked heavy to wear, and I wondered how anyone could. I wandered through the area, realizing this ball I loved had started all the way back in the fourteenth century. It had a notorious past; a king had been murdered under disguise at a masquerade ball, but aside from that, it had become a way for people to live out their lustful dreams without others finding out.

Apparently, these balls weren't so popular anymore, but not to me. I loved the costumes and extravagant masks, as well as the gaiety. It was like everyone felt safe behind their anonymity. It was thrilling.

I stopped to look at a mask that cupped your forehead and the top part of your head. It was gilded in gold lines and had a series of jewels running along the edges. It had a deep, ruby red velvet finish around the eyeholes, and I wondered what it felt like to wear it. I was just about to put it on when I felt a tap on my shoulder.

I looked up to see a slender-built man in a simple black mask. His eyes were dark and inviting, and I knew I was a goner already.

"Are you alone?" he asked me.

"I am," I said, not sure why I trusted this guy to tell him that. His eyes reminded me of Luc's, and part of me secretly hoped this was him. But he didn't smell like Luc, sound like Luc, or even carry himself like Luc. Nor was there that confidence or smoldering hotness exuding from his body. This guy was just sexy, that was it. But he was close enough, and I had promised myself that I would have fun tonight, so I would take what was offered.

"Care to dance, then?" he now asked with a slight grin.

"Sure."

He offered his hand in the most gentleman-like way, and I placed mine in his. As he walked us toward the ballroom, I did a quick scan of the entryway as we passed by and was glad to see Becca and Brandon weren't there anymore. They must be inside dancing. I was happy for Becca, even if she didn't want to admit it to herself.

As soon as we entered the ballroom, he swept me into his arms. With one arm extended, he held onto one of my hands, while the other came down to the small of my back and pulled me in. I was so close I could see the stubble on his chin. His lips were luscious, and when he caught me staring at them, he swept his tongue along his bottom lip. I swear my innards turned molten hot.

A gasp escaped me when he pulled me in even closer. He was twirling me around the ballroom among all the other guests, and I was having the time of my life. I hadn't enjoyed myself this much in years—it was exhilarating!

Just as we finished a round of the ballroom, another guy cut in and proceeded to dance me around the room. And then another, and then another. However, the first guy always came back to dance with me in between dances. We never talked, nor did we ask each other's names, but I swear he held me closer every time we danced. A small part of me relished the feeling of being desired.

Becca had stopped by a couple of times to make sure I was okay, and the smile that she left with made me happy. She knew I was clearly enjoying myself and was congratulating herself on a job well done. She'd managed to pull me from my empty apartment for a night out for the second time in three weeks. I owed her for it and knew I should take her out for a treat this week. I recalled a little boutique in town that she was always talking about. It would be the perfect place to take her to say thank you.

Decision made, I smiled at my dance partner, realizing we were now dancing toward the staircase. He stopped and gestured at it. "I'd like to show you something. Would you care to follow me?"

The look he gave me almost made me buckle at the knees. "Okay," I said, and I was embarrassed at how breathless I sounded.

He must have noticed because a smirk crossed his lips. He led me up the stairs, and the whole time I followed him my heart was racing while my mind repeated over and over not to trip over my dress and make a complete fool of myself.

When we got to the second floor, there were quite a few people around. They were mingling or necking with their masks still on. We weaved between a few couples before he led me into a room. It was well-lit, and surprisingly, it was not a bedroom but more of a sitting room. There was a couple already inside, but as soon as they saw us they left. I looked over at my guy, thinking he must have some sway for people to move that quickly around him. He was definitely the silent, mysterious type.

"Wait here. I'm going to go get something," he now said.

"Okay."

As soon as he disappeared into the connecting room, the

magic stopped. It was too quiet, and my imagination started going wild as reality began to catch up. This wasn't right. What crazy person followed a stranger to a private room where no one else knew where she was?

I had done it again—trapped myself. How stupid could I get?

I turned and started walking toward the door. That's when I heard footsteps; they sounded heavier than the guy I'd come up here with.

"Leaving so soon?"

It was a voice that sent chills up my spine, freezing my heart. It was all I could do to continue breathing. I could not faint and be at his mercy! What did I do? What could I do? *This wasn't happening! This couldn't be happening! How did he find me?* Becca had said I was safe in this town—it was a small town, where everyone knew everyone else. *Becca! I have to get back to Becca!* My mind was racing, and my feet seemed unable to move. I felt helpless and trapped.

"I've missed you," he now said.

With that admission, I realized it was too late to run.

A hand touched my arm, and I shuddered. I used to love his touch . . . until it became too strong. Until makeup couldn't cover up what was best hidden.

"Have you missed *me*?" he pushed, his hand tightening on my arm.

He slowly turned me toward him. He had a bird mask on. Its beak was so long it hung below his chin. The mask covered his whole face, but I knew it was him. I could feel his energy wafting over me, threatening to take over my senses once again. Once upon a time, I'd thought I was lucky, that he was the best man I could ever have. The one who would take care of me forever. I was wrong. So, so wrong.

Somehow, I was able to find my voice. "Why are you here?"

"Same as you, sweetheart—to enjoy the ball, to dance and be merry."

I felt his hand skimming up and down my arm, and I wanted to run, but my brain had disconnected from my feet. Then his fingers closed around my arm and squeezed it with a bit of force. Panic surged through me.

His mouth tightened. "Why did you leave? I know you said a bunch of words that day, but I know you didn't mean it, Jill. I'm here to bring you home. You've had enough time to calm down."

Bring me home? He knew I'd been hiding here all along? *Oh goodness, I need to get out of here! I need to find Becca!*

The door suddenly burst open behind me, and a group of girls came rushing in, laughing and having a merry time. When they saw us, they started excusing themselves, but the abruptness of their entrance was all I needed to jumpstart my feet again. My movement startled Rich, and his hold loosened.

I made a run for it, pushing through the girls. I heard curses flung my way, shortly followed by dull thuds as Rich came through the door after me, not caring whom he shoved to the ground. Did I really mean that much to him that he wanted me back? Or was he just mad at me for leaving him? All I knew for sure was that I did not want to find out.

He caught me just as I got to the top of the stairs, but I was ready for him and stomped my heel into his foot. He cried out in pain, much to my satisfaction, and I quickly turned to continue down the stairs. I felt pressure at the back of my dress just before I heard something rip. He'd grabbed onto the ruching!

Cool air hit my skin where the seam had come undone. The action left me unbalanced, and I tripped over my dress, twisting my ankle and banging my head on the banister. I felt something sharp pierce my face underneath the mask, but I told myself there was no time to check. Thankfully, the hand that came to help me was not Rich's but another guest whom I had run into on my way down.

I glanced behind me to see Rich glaring down at me, his hands curled into fists. We held each other's eyes for a moment before his flicked up to the people around me. In the next moment he retreated, disappearing into the crowd. I didn't wait to see if he was coming back. I turned and thanked the people around me, who clearly thought I'd had a bit too much to drink, and hobbled the rest of the way down the stairs.

I didn't bother looking for Becca or Brandon, instead making a direct beeline for the entrance. I asked the front desk attendants to call a cab, but only after I made them take off their masks so I could inspect their faces. All I saw were teenagers scared of the crazed lady inspecting them. They told me there were no cabs tonight as everyone was at the party, but that one of them could drive me home instead. I took the offer.

I stood out in the open where the ushers could see me and waited and waited and waited. I thought my heart would come up into my throat, and I couldn't stop my hands from shaking.

Rich had found me. He was back. There was no running away—ever. He would always find me. I had to go home and pack, because there was no way I was going back to him. I would keep running from him for the rest of my life if that's what it took. I couldn't tell Becca, I couldn't get her involved again. I couldn't do that to her after what she'd just been through with me.

When a car pulled up with one of the teenage boys in the driver's seat, I rushed inside without waiting for anyone to hold the door open for me.

The drive home was tense. When we got back to the apartments, I went to grab my clutch to pay and realized I didn't have it. In the midst of everything, I had dropped it. It was probably still at the ball. I groaned and leaned back in my seat, crying.

The tears must have scared the boy because he immediately started assuring me that it was okay. He knew who I was, and I could pay him later, he said. I didn't question how he knew me, but I let him mollify me and exited the car. He peeled away from the curb so fast I knew he was relieved to leave the crazy lady behind.

As I stood there on the pavement, I realized that without my clutch I didn't have my apartment key. That meant I would have to find Miti and ask her for a spare key . . . except Miti had gone on a trip, and I couldn't face asking anyone else right now. Which meant there was only one place I could go.

I headed into the lobby, happy to see it empty, and took the elevator to the garage. Being a forgetful person, I had stuck my second set of car keys in the wheelhouse. After finding the key, I slid into the driver's seat and cried. This was it. He would find me here in my car and take me back with him. To do what, I didn't dare imagine.

This was what I got for having hope.

LUC

JILL HAD SMELLED DIVINE. Every part of me was screaming to go with her to the ball. To be there by her side and dance with her for the whole night. I knew she wanted that too. Her heartbeat had pounded like drummers in a marching band, calling me to follow, and my wolf was screaming at me to go. But it wasn't right to do so; I couldn't lead her on.

"You brought us here to intimidate her, didn't you?" Bruno said, giving me a shove.

I looked up and growled at him before stalking into the living room.

"We don't like being used like that," Jacob called after me.

"Back off you two!" This was all a mistake. Everything. I shouldn't have asked them to come here. I knew they'd give me a hard time, but maybe if this plan worked, listening to them complain would be worth it.

"She's your fated mate," Jacob stated.

"No she isn't," I growled, turning to look at them.

They were both standing in front of me with their arms

crossed over their chests. I saw them give each other a look, and I knew they wouldn't back down till I told them what was going on. But what was there to tell? I was having feelings that I shouldn't be having, that was all.

"You know I already fated with Kit, and she left me. It's not going to happen again."

"You're so dense sometimes, you know that? You never acted like this with Kit. Mom's right; she should really take a rock over your head to knock some sense into you."

I glared at him. That was a low blow bringing Mom into this. "You two should head home. I shouldn't have asked you to come."

"Nah, we're staying tonight. Haven't seen you in a while. You might as well tell us about this girl."

I groaned, realizing there was no way I was getting out of this. "There's nothing to tell. She moved in here a month ago. Took Kit's old room. She's been a great neighbor and tenant. No parties, no loud noises, and hasn't complained about the howling when we're running in the woods. That's it, nothing more."

"I call BS on that," Bruno said. "You want to know what I think?"

"No, I don't."

Bruno ignored me. "I think you're dying inside and are itching to follow after her to make sure she's safe, because if anything *did* happen to her, you would never forgive yourself."

"You know, being our big brother, we look up to you and follow closely whatever you do," Jacob added.

"I hate you both." I stormed into my room, unable to listen to them anymore and not wanting to admit they were right.

My tux was in the very back of my closet. I hadn't used it

in years, not since Mom decided she didn't want to hold any more fancy parties. She said that would be up to me and my spouse moving forward, as she was going to retire and live a happy life in the woods. When I told her that the closest I would ever come to hosting a ball was the community center parties Brandon and I put on, it only made her smile at me, which annoyed me even more.

I changed into my tux and looked in the mirror. It wouldn't hurt to just stop by and check on Jill; she didn't have to know I was there. I groaned, knowing I would have to deal with Brandon when I got there, but just a glimpse of Jill would be enough to calm my wolf down—even just a smell or the sound of her heartbeat. *A taste would be even better....*

A rumble went through my throat at the thought, and I couldn't get changed fast enough. I had to be there now! The thought of others putting their hands on her when it could have been me had me rushing through the finishing touches, making me tear the first bow tie I tried to put on.

"You're going to blow a fuse if your heart rate goes any faster," Bruno called from the other room.

I could hear them laughing through the bedroom wall. *Don't answer him. It's exactly what he wants.* I finished dressing and stormed out of the room, clobbering them both across the head.

"Hey! We're just messing with you. We're on your side," Jacob yelled, grabbing my arm and pulling me into a headlock and mussing up my hair. "Now you don't look too serious," he announced, letting me go with a satisfied smirk.

I stormed out of the apartment with their laughter trailing behind me.

It didn't take me long to get to the family mansion. It was situated on the top of the highest hill in town and belonged to my great-great-grandfather, though no one in the family lived there anymore. Grandfather was the last of us to live in it. Mother used to throw her balls there, but since she'd retired a committee of humans had taken over, running them about four times a year. There wasn't much excitement in this small town, so we all loved having a big get-together when the occasion arose.

I parked the car under a tree I used to climb when I was a boy. The entrance was quiet now that everyone had arrived, but I could hear music and voices floating out the doors. There was something in the air, a scent I had smelled before but couldn't place.

I nodded at the man taking tickets at the entrance. He knew my family and let me in without asking. I chuckled at the thought that Brandon came with actual tickets; he'd tried to make it look official in front of the women.

As soon as I entered the mansion, the scent I'd detected was immediately replaced by the aroma of fine perfumes. One circle of the lobby had me politely saying no to multiple dance card offers. I didn't want to dance with anyone but Jill; she was why I was here.

I walked into the ballroom and spotted Brandon deep in conversation with Becca. Why the two of them didn't just call each other a couple was beyond me. Brandon had never fated before, and Becca was a lovely person. There was no reason to not follow through with it, apart from his weak excuse that he liked to be "free." I shook my head and walked toward them.

"Luc! You made it. I knew you'd come to your senses," Brandon said, pulling me in for a big hug. He was the touchy-feely brother. Mom always said he gave the best cuddles.

"Can I talk to you for a second?"

"Of course," he said, giving me a raised eyebrow.

"In private."

He turned to Becca. "If you'll excuse me."

She gave a nod and a smile, and I could feel her eyes on us as we walked away.

Brandon followed me outside into the still night air, where there were a few people congregating. We didn't have this many people in the town, and I wondered where all of them came from.

"Did you smell something when you came in?" I asked Brandon.

"You mean the smell of perfumes?"

"No!" I brushed my hand through my hair.

He gave me an odd look but thankfully didn't push me. "I think I smelled something off, but you know how my sense of smell is. It's not what it used to be."

I rubbed my hands down my face, suddenly realizing I had asked Brandon the one question he couldn't answer. "I'm sorry. I'm so wound up, I wasn't thinking."

"No problem. Your girl is inside looking at the masks on the wall, the ones that Mom says she's never giving away because they belong in the family."

"The ones that gave us nightmares growing up?"

"Those are the ones."

"Great."

Brandon clapped me on the shoulder. "Have fun tonight, you deserve it. You've been so tense lately, Luc. Let loose. Dad's still alpha, and you can just enjoy life right now."

"Easy for the non-firstborn to say."

"I'm only a year behind you. And technically, you're not the firstborn, Sandy is."

I growled. "You know what I mean."

Brandon ignored my comment. "And I miss my brother. We used to go out on the town all the time."

"I know and I'm sorry."

"Go and find Jill and have fun. Go dance."

He turned me to face the ballroom and would have given me a shove, but I didn't want my little brother telling me what to do anymore. I needed to keep some sort of dominance over him. I made myself walk back into the ballroom at the same time Becca walked out.

"Oh, Luc, Jill's by the masks," she said in passing.

"Yes, I heard."

She stopped suddenly and placed a hand on my arm. "Can I ask you a favor?"

"Yes . . . ." Becca had never asked me for a favor before.

"Brandon didn't eat dinner tonight because he was running late to meet me, but I know he's starving. Do you mind if we go out to eat now that you're here? I don't want to leave Jill on her own without knowing anyone's here for her."

Brandon has no idea how good he has it. "Of course, you two go. I'm here now."

"Thank you!"

I continued walking through the throngs of people, who were all laughing and dancing and having a merry time. The atmosphere was starting to rub off on me and memories of us as kids running around the hallways peeking into the ballroom came back. We used to rush and hide if a grown-up came to see what the noise was about.

I knew every nook and cranny in this house, but it was so big that it was non-personal. I liked my apartment a lot better. The museum Mom had curated was in front of me, and I could see the crowd of people by the masks.

Jill's heartbeat was strong and content, and my body loosened at the sound of it. She was mine. My wolf knew it, but I couldn't bear the thought of her breaking my heart.

I decided to watch her from the sideline and make sure she stayed safe. I ventured into the gallery and saw her immediately. Her black hair blended in with her dress and mask, and in contrast, her skin glowed with warmth. She was all I could focus on. No one else mattered. Her heartbeat was calm, and I found my feet moving toward her of their own accord.

But wait! Who was that man with her? My fists clenched at my sides, and I drew in a breath before reminding myself that she didn't know I was there. We weren't an item, and she had no loyalty to me.

. . . But the sight of his hand reaching out to take hers, and then Jill readily giving herself over to him for what looked like a dance, sent my heart racing. My body felt primed for a fight. I could feel my muscles rippling under my skin as I followed them into the ballroom.

I watched as he gathered her in his arms and twirled her around the room. Just as I was about to go and separate them, I saw Jill smile. It was the brightest thing I'd seen in a long time. She looked so happy compared to how I had left her. Who was I to tell her who she could or couldn't dance with? I had no claim over her.

I took a deep breath and walked to the bar, content on hearing her heartbeat and knowing she was okay. I'd catch the next dance; no need to burst her bubble just yet.

By the time I came back, though, she was already dancing with another man, and she was absolutely glowing and having the time of her life. Then the first guy came back again, and she readily let him pull her against him and dance to the next song too.

My heart couldn't take this. I was a fool to have come here. She was perfectly fine without me. Why in the world did I let my brothers get to me? They knew nothing about love or how much it hurt to be left behind, to be discarded like you had never meant anything to that person. I'd vowed I wouldn't let a girl do that to me ever again. Yet here I was . . . .

I turned and left. She'd be just fine. No side-stop at an ice cream parlor tonight. No chance of looking into dark warm eyes and luscious lips that had the cutest pout when she was thinking. My wolf was clawing to get out, and I would let it. There was no need for me to be here anymore—no reason for me to have ever come!

I ran toward the woods and shifted, howling a lone tune as soon as I was deep into the trees.

LUC

THE RUN through the woods was just what I needed—fresh air, quiet, and best of all, none of my brothers ribbing me. It should have been calming, except it wasn't. A nagging feeling had started to grate at my nerves. It was telling me to go back. I shook my head, telling myself there was nothing back there for me. Jill was better off without me. Broken and unsettled by relationships, I could never be what she needed.

But the feeling wouldn't go away. It lingered on like a bad smell . . . just like that odd scent I'd detected when I arrived at the mansion. Something was wrong, very wrong.

I ran back to the ball as fast as I could. It seemed the woods were never-ending, and when I got back, people were starting to leave. I nodded at people I knew as I weaved in and out of guests in the ballroom, looking for Jill. But I didn't see her, and I wasn't able to find her heartbeat among the remaining guests. I next looked for Brandon and Becca, but it appeared they had not returned.

That tingling sensation had muted, but it hadn't gone away, telling me something still wasn't right. I did one last sweep of the ballroom before running to my car to head home.

I drove like a mad wolf desperate to get back to his mate, slamming the steering wheel and cursing myself for not staying at the ball. If Jill was hurt, there would be a price to pay.

The drive seemed to go on forever. I pulled into the garage and willed myself to take some deep breaths, trying to calm my heart rate down before heading upstairs. If I didn't, I might just charge straight to her room to make sure she was okay, and I knew if I did that I'd scare her away for sure. She would move out immediately, too afraid to show her face in front of me again. I couldn't have that. If I couldn't have her, at least I would watch over her while she lived in my building.

After I calmed down, I got out of my car and started for the elevator, passing her car on the way. A slight shadow caught my attention, and I turned to look straight at her car. What I saw inside made all my breathing exercises fall to the wayside. She was slumped in the front seat, still in her ballgown.

I ran to the car and put my hands on the window. I yelled Jill's name. She didn't even stir when I banged on the glass. Without thinking, I pulled one arm back and slammed it into the window. A big spiderweb formed on impact. I suddenly realized that if I hit the window again glass would fall on Jill. I quickly ran to the other side of the car and took out the passenger window, then I reached inside to unlock the door.

I could hear her heart pounding in a regular rhythm as I sank into the seat beside her. It calmed me down a little—until I gently pushed her head back so that it was resting on the headrest. That was when I noticed the gash above her right eye. I slammed my hand against the dashboard, shaking the whole car. Jill stirred a bit, and I immediately regretted my action, but thankfully she did not awaken.

Assessing her further, I saw that she had dried blood on her head and feet, and a series of bruises that were fast appearing on her face, legs, and arm. A deep growl escaped my chest, and I didn't care who heard it. I was seeing red, and it was only because she was right in front of me that I didn't smash our surroundings to smithereens.

I exited the vehicle and walked around to open the driver's door. Gently placing my hands behind her back and legs, I lifted her out. My first thought was that she was as light as a feather. I could carry her all day and wouldn't mind a second of it. My arms curled around her tightly, and I felt her snuggle closer into me. A sense of possessiveness washed over me then, and I closed my eyes, allowing the feelings to pass through. Even during the best of times with Kit, I had never remotely felt anything like I now felt for Jill.

Thankfully, no bones seemed to be broken, and her breathing was even. That calmed me down enough to start walking toward the elevator.

The elevator doors opened as I approached. It was quite a sight when Jacob, Bruno, Damon, and Brent poured out. Seeing Jill in my arms, they immediately rushed over.

"We heard you growl and came to see what happened," Bruno said.

"I don't know what's happened," I snapped. "I found her like this in her car. I'm taking her upstairs, so move over." I realized I was being a bit gruff when they had only come down to help, but all I could think about was how I needed to attend to Jill.

"Shouldn't we take her to the hospital? She could be really hurt," Jacob asked.

"No!" The memory of what Jill had said about her ex working at the hospital made me hesitant to take her there. "I'll have someone come here if we need to. Now move over."

The guys moved out of my way so I could enter the elevator with Jill in my arms, and we went upstairs and headed to her room. Once there, Jacob tried the handle, only to find it was locked. Of course, it was locked. I had heard it myself when she had left earlier tonight—when I had been a douchebag and let her go alone.

Growling, I turned to head to my room. "Brent, search the car and see if you can find her purse," I called over my shoulder. "I didn't see it, but it might have fallen under her seat."

While Brent ran for the stairs, Damon opened my door, and I immediately went in and placed Jill on my bed before unbuttoning her coat. As soon as her coat was open, I slid it off and noticed that the bottom half of her dress was ripped, showcasing her beautifully smooth legs. Before I could focus on her legs too much, I noticed the edge of the split was ragged. I bent over and took a closer look, and all the guys jumped when I grabbed the remote on the bedside table and threw it across the room, barely constraining the roar that threatened to come out of my mouth. That tear proclaimed that someone had been pawing at her and that she must have fought back! It could only mean one thing—whoever it was had attacked her without her permission, which was a big no-no for me and anyone in my pack, much less a stranger when it came to my mate.

Bruno brought blankets from the guest closet, and I was thankful I had my brothers here to help out. I didn't bother looking at their faces, though, as I knew I'd see pity written across them. They were aware I was blaming myself for what had happened.

Brent came in and said, "Boss, there's no purse in the car."

I slammed my hand on the coffee table, which elicited a jolt from Jill. I reached out and rubbed a hand across her temple and down her hair in a soothing motion. As the smooth strands ran through my fingers, I realized that this was where I belonged—with Jill. Nowhere else. How was I crazy enough to think I could avoid her? She was my everything. My mate.

My wolf purred at the thought, relaxing now that I finally

agreed with him instead of pushing against the inevitable. This feeling was nothing like what I had felt for Kit. I knew that if I lost Jill, that would be the end of me.

"Luc, is there anything you want us to do? Damon has already gone out to smell the perimeter and see if there was anyone lurking here," Jacob said.

"You won't find anyone here. Call Brandon. Tell him he needs to come over."

I had a bad feeling I knew who had done this to Jill, and he wasn't going to get to her again, even if I had to hunt him down and tear him limb from limb myself.

"You should really get some sleep," Jacob announced.

"I did sleep!" I hadn't meant to snap at Jacob, but what was I supposed to do?

"For thirty minutes," Jacob shot back.

"Just let it go. How am I supposed to sleep when she still hasn't woken up yet?"

"It's four in the morning; she will probably sleep through till at least nine."

I glared at him because he was making too much sense. "I'm going for a run."

I got up to leave, but he interjected with something we'd been arguing about for most of the night. "If the scent you smelled is from someone looking to attack us, you should really let Dad know so we can bring the whole pack in."

I didn't want to hear it. "Just watch over her while I'm gone," I growled, continuing toward the door.

"Don't do anything stupid, Luc. You can't help her if you're dead."

"I'm only running around the complex," I ground out.

I slammed the door on the way out and caught it just in time before it banged after remembering Jill was asleep.

Seeing Jill lying there on the bed tore my heart into pieces. I should have been at the ball! I ran deep into the woods and howled, letting out all my pent-up energy and nervousness. Something wasn't right. I had been unsettled since I smelled that faint whiff of familiarity at the ball. I knew the smell was related to what happened to Jill, I just couldn't figure out why. Running had made my emotions somewhat feasible to control, but I couldn't keep running. I had to figure this out so Jill didn't get hurt again.

JILL

I WOKE up with a throbbing headache and told myself I shouldn't have enjoyed myself as much as I had last night. Then, flashbacks of the ball started replaying in my mind in slow motion, and the horrors of last night washed over me. My eyes popped open, and I realized I was in an unfamiliar place. It smelled different, too, like masculinity on steroids. I couldn't be back in Rich's room!

I immediately sat up and glanced around, looking for the familiar dresser and bookshelves Rich had installed to entice me to stay put. Gifts were his go-to. Tricks, as I saw them now; nothing more than tricks to get me to stay. And I was stupid enough to fall for them—but not now.

What I saw, though, made me pause. This room was not Rich's, and I only knew that because it was cluttered. In a good way, though, as the room felt homey and welcoming. A knitted blanket was laid over me, and there were real books on the shelf—some I recognized from grade school—along with trinkets collected from around the world. There was a television mounted on the wall with photos hanging next to it, containing photos of *actual* people. Rich would never have done that. He would have called it baseless, unworthy of his time. If he wanted to see people, he'd go see them he'd say; why hang them on the wall?

But then a worse thought came to mind—maybe this was all a trick? It wouldn't be the first time Rich had changed my environment to make me confused and further keep me in his grasp.

I jumped up, on high alert. The place was quiet; this was the perfect chance to escape. I had to try. Now that I'd tasted freedom, I was never going to stick with him again. I wouldn't. Becca had saved me, and I deserved a life free of imprisonment.

I jumped off the bed, only to have my legs give out, knocking over the drink I hadn't seen on the side table in the process. I cursed, thinking now I'd done it. Rich would find a stain on his table and carpet, and I would get a beating for it. I grabbed the first thing I could find—the blanket—and started wiping up the mess.

The door opened behind me, startling me, and I turned, fully expecting Rich to be staring at me with a "gotcha" look on his face. It would serve me right for believing I had the freedom to do as I pleased.

But those thoughts came to a halt when I found it was Luc staring back at me, without a shirt on, and his pants hanging low on his hips. He looked startled himself, with his hair going every which way.

"Jill," he rasped.

Luc started walking toward me, and that's when I bolted. Memories started surfacing of the men who came out of their rooms, all who looked like Luc, as if they were in a gang just like Rich. I had left one only to join another! *No, no, no, no, no, no!*

I ran out of the bedroom and straight toward the front

door. My fingers curved around the handle when a massive hand pressed against mine and held the door shut.

"Jill—"

"No, please don't hurt me! I just want to go! Please, just let me go, Luc! I won't tell anyone about you, I promise I won't tell a soul. Just let me go back to my room. I'll pack and be out of your hair before you know it. You won't ever see me again, I promise." The words rambled out of my mouth as I sank to the floor. I covered my head with my hands and hoped I would only receive bruises instead of ending up in the emergency room.

There was a knock on the door, followed by a voice that sounded like Damon's. "Boss, everything okay?"

"Everything is fine. Tell the boys to go back to their rooms." Luc's voice sounded gruffer than normal, and I knew my time was numbered. Rich's voice always dropped an octave the madder he got. The longer he yelled at me, the deeper it went till it was nothing but a guttural growl.

There wasn't any verbal acknowledgment of Luc's order, but I heard the doors open and close.

"Jill."

He crouched down next to me and then a hand touched my arm. I was curled up so tight. I wished he'd just get it over with already. This was torture. What did he want with me?

A moment later his hand was gone. "I'm not going to hurt you, Jill. Please, open your eyes. I'm in the living room. You're free to open the door and leave if you want."

It was a trick. As soon as I opened my eyes, a fist would be there to knock me senseless. But Luc's voice had come from a few feet away, and so far no blow had landed. I peeked between my arms and, sure enough, there was no one in front of me or beside me. I leaned back and felt the door to the coat closet along my spine. I then turned to face the living room and saw Luc sitting on the floor, with his back leaning against the sofa. He was breathing hard, and I could tell he was worked up about something.

"I'm sorry I spilled the water. I'll replace the table and the carpet with whatever you want."

"You're worried about what you spilled?" Confusion lit his face, and I started to point back toward his bedroom, but then he said slowly, "You're hurt and you care about spilling some water on the table?"

"It must have damaged the—"

"Who did this to you?" he barked.

"What?"

"You heard me. Who made you so scared? Who hurt you yesterday?"

I blinked at him. "You know?"

"You're covered in cuts and bruises and your dress is torn."

I looked down to see that he was right. My dress was torn, and I had welts on my arm and legs, probably from where Rich had grabbed me and then when I'd fallen. "It's nothing you need to be concerned about."

"Not be concerned . . . ! Are you serious?"

I finally began to believe that he really wasn't going to hurt me, and I stood up to leave.

Luc put up a hand. "What are you doing? We need to get you to a doctor."

"What?! No!" My heart rate instantly spiked, and I started wondering if Luc was in cahoots with Rich. Had I walked out of the lion's den only to fall right into another?

"I know you said you don't like going to hospitals, but you're hurt, and I won't let him near you," he repeated.

"No, please. Please don't send me back to him. What do you want? What is Rich giving you? Maybe I could offer something better."

"Rich?" A growl came out of his throat. It was so deep that I jumped, hitting my back against the door.

"Rich is his name?" he repeated. His face had become a vision of pure hatred.

"Yes . . . . He's a . . . he's a plastic surgeon at the hospital in the city. That's why I can't go. Please don't send me back to him—I'll do anything!" I started sinking to the floor again, my legs unable to hold me upright, fear once again riding my spine. I did not want to be under Rich's control again.

A pause fell between us. I wasn't sure what to do. Should I try to open the door and run for it? He did tell me to go. My senses were all over the place; telling me to leave *now*, but also wary that Luc would chase me and lock me away. Although, the longer the pause, the less I thought he'd do the latter.

Then Luc did the worst thing he could have done—he punched the wall so hard his hand went right through the plaster. The suddenness of the action and the loud noise that ensued made me scream, and this time I did go for the handle and make a run for it. However, he was at the door before I could blink, yelling for Damon and Brent. Four burly men instantly came out of various rooms.

"Brent, escort Jill back into my place, and stand guard at her door. I don't want anyone coming or going from the room. Damon, go outside and secure the perimeter. The rest of you come with me. We have a little visit to pay a certain someone."

"No," I cried. "Please don't lock me in your room! Please . . ." But he didn't hear me; they were already through the door and running down the stairs.

I looked at Brent, and his look of concern was somewhat reassuring. There was no ruthless need to hurt me in his expression. "Brent—" I began.

"Don't try to run. We have to follow orders," he said quickly, cutting me off.

My shoulders drooped. I'd heard that before, but if I was going to be locked away, I'd rather be at my place. I started walking to my room, but Brent put a hand on my shoulder. I instantly tensed, and he dropped his hand as if burned.

"You can't go back to your place," he said slowly. "We couldn't find your purse, and Miti's spare keys have been missing this week." He seemed to tense up at that. "It's for your own safety."

I'd heard that before too. Giving in, I marched myself back into Luc's room. At least I was by myself this time. Brent stayed outside and watched me as I closed the door on my fate.

LUC

"You two go walk around the perimeter while I go in," I ordered Bruno and Damon.

"Shouldn't you wait for Brandon?" Bruno asked.

"He's been unreachable all night. No, I'm going to find out who this Rich guy is right now."

"Luc—"

I shot Bruno a look and pointed to the side of the building. "Go!" A scowl formed on their faces, but they obeyed.

Jill's slip was the goldmine I had been waiting for. Whoever this Rich guy was, he would pay for what he'd done to Jill. Aside from Jill, I'd only seen one other woman who was so scared for her life that she would pledge to do *anything* to save herself. I had vowed to my sister after we tore her captives apart that we would never let something like this happen to her again. The same would go for Jill.

I now knew without a doubt she was my mate. My one and only. And if this Rich guy had hurt her like Pac had hurt our sister, Sandy, he would be in for a world of hurt.

I was halfway to the hospital when I realized this was a bad idea. When we brought Sandy here, I'd quickly learned how protective the nurses were. It was comforting to see, but I knew they would never let me in to see Rich if he was here, as my anger was worse now. I stomped back to the car and met up with the boys.

Having found Rich's picture on the hospital site with no problem, we knew he'd be coming out of or into the building at some point. We waited for what seemed like an eternity before spotting him walking out of the main entrance. He had a bag in hand and was heading in our direction. He was of a bigger build than I expected, and the way he walked had a certain familiarity to it.

A growl at my back had me turning. Jacob was leaning out the side window in the back and sniffing the air. "What is it?" I asked him.

"It's him."

I felt like snarling. "We can see that. Are all of you ready to grab him?"

Jacob let out another growl. "Stay put! We can't go out and grab him."

I whirled on him. "What do you mean? This is the guy who hurt Jill! I'm going to—"

"You don't recognize his smell?" Jacob demanded.

By this time, Bruno had also sniffed the air and was looking at Jacob with incredulous eyes. "You really think it's him?"

"Who?!" I slammed my hands on the dashboard. "He's going to be gone by the time you all decide to help me. Who's the eldest here, anyways?!"

"You are, but we're also your family, and I say we tell Dad. You're going to need reinforcements," Jacob said.

"Duck!" Bruno cried, pressing my head down hard as we all lowered our heads below the windshield.

"What the heck are you doing? Let me go!" I snarled.

But Bruno ignored me, only letting me go after peering out the window again.

"What in the world was that for?" I yelled at him.

"I think he saw us," Jacob said.

"There's no way, unless he's a wolf as well, and you still haven't told me who he is!" I snapped at him.

I was ready to pull my brothers apart when Jacob said, "It's Pac."

"What about Pac?" I snapped. "He was banished years ago."

"That man, Rich, is Pac," Jacob now said slowly.

"How would you know that?"

"I remember from when Sandy was with him. We would all smell like sweat and dirt, but he always smelled of gardenias. How can you not smell him?"

I closed my eyes and willed my heartrate to slow down. If what Jacob said was true, my anger was getting the better of me and blocking more of my senses than I cared to admit.

"You guys used to tell me Mom hated him, but Dad loved him. Are you sure it's the same Pac?" Bruno said, leaning his head out to see where Rich—or Pac—was going.

I growled, hitting the steering wheel. All I wanted to do was go out, grab Rich, and pummel him till he understood that he could never harm Jill again. But if this really was Pac, there was more at play here than we thought.

I tightened my fists but couldn't deny that we needed to look into this further. I couldn't put Jill in more danger; I needed to know what was really going on. "All right, but you better be right about this Jacob or Dad will have our hides. Follow him to see where he lives. Bruno, notify Dad."

"Luc, she's been putting up a fight. She says she needs to go to work or she'll lose her job," Brent warned as I stepped up to the front door of my apartment. "Plus, I'm starting to wonder if the missing keys have something to do with all this too."

"I'll talk to her," I said gruffly. "And you know Miti can't control when she shifts anymore. When she does, she goes missing for days on end and can't remember a thing. She probably took the keys with her. I'm sure it's unrelated." I didn't wait for Brent to respond before I stomped into my apartment.

I stopped in my tracks when I spotted Jill sitting on the couch. She was staring right at me as if steeling herself to talk to me.

Fire was burning inside of me. Couldn't she tell I was worried, and that staying here was for her own good? I was about to tell her as much when Becca came storming up behind me and almost knocked me over.

She whirled on me and said, "How dare you! If you weren't Brandon's brother, I'd throw a lawsuit on you so fast you wouldn't know what hit you! How dare you keep my friend under lock and key!"

Brandon was now standing by my side and trying to calm Becca down. "Becca, I don't think he knows what happened to Jill."

This time I whirled on him. "What happened to Jill? And where were you all night?"

"I think Jill should tell you what happened herself, and last night I went to dinner with Becca like we told you."

"That was hours ago!"

I saw an exchange of looks between Becca and Brandon and was about to follow up on that when Jill piped in.

"I'm right here, you know!" She made her way over to me. "What you're doing to me right now is exactly what Rich used to do to me. He kept me under house arrest, never to see or talk to anyone out of pure jealousy."

"That's not—" I started, but she held up a hand to stop me.

"I'm not done yet. I'm leaving. I have work. That's the end of our discussion."

"She's coming with me." Becca put her arm around Jill and literally pulled her around me, while I stood there wondering what the heck was going on. My wolf was scratching at me to stop them and make Jill stay, but Brandon had a hand on my arm that I wasn't going to escape from. Fine, I'd let her go, but Jill was a fool if she thought I wouldn't continue to watch over her.

I signaled for Brent to follow the ladies, adding, "And find Damon to go with you."

He nodded and headed for the stairs.

Brandon held onto me until we heard the elevator close and start heading down. I punched him as soon as he let me go. "What the heck, Brandon!" I exclaimed.

"That was uncalled for!" he said, taking a swing at me too. "We left you at the ball last night, only to wake up this morning to multiple phone calls from Jacob and Bruno that there had been an emergency, and Becca and I needed to come home immediately. I should be asking you what the heck happened?"

"And you should have been here earlier! You saw Jill. She's all bruised and cut up! And we just found out who her ex is."

Jacob had just come back and decided he wanted in on the conversation now. "Yeah! Rich is Pac! He's been hiding right under our noses this whole time!"

Brandon got defensive very quickly after hearing this. "What . . . do . . . you . . . mean . . . Pac . . . has . . . been . . . hiding . . . under . . . our . . . noses?" He was breathing heavily, and it was my turn to put a hand on his arm in case he flew off his rockers.

Jacob backed up at seeing Brandon get fired up. Of all our brothers, Brandon was always the happy-go-lucky one. Nothing bothered him. Nothing except Pac. It was Brandon who was with Sandy the night Pac attacked her. But Brandon hadn't been able to help her, because he had been knocked out from the very beginning. Sandy had been whisked away until our whole pack went and brought her back. Dad was never hard on Brandon because of what happened, but Brandon never forgave himself.

Keeping a steady hand on his arm, I said, "Brandon, Bruno has already gone to notify Dad. We're getting the whole pack together now."

JILL

"I know you two are behind us!" I called back, having seen Damon and Brent following at a distance. Being with Rich had taught me a thing or two about surveying my surroundings. Shop windows and car mirrors were my friends.

"Who's behind us?" Becca asked. She turned to look, and sure enough, Damon and Brent were walking toward us, not bothering to stay hidden anymore now their ruse was up. "What in the world are you two doing here?" she demanded.

"We're making sure Jill is safe," Bruno explained.

"I'm perfectly fine, thank you very much. I do not need you two tailing me everywhere I go." I hooked my arm through Becca's for stability. I sounded braver than I thought I would.

Clearly, Damon thought so as well. "It doesn't hurt to have us around. We don't have to be near you. We'll just follow at a discrete distance. I'm surprised you even knew we were here."

"Years of my ex dodging people taught me some tricks."

Damon and Brent exchanged a look. I didn't know what that was about, and I didn't want to know.

Brent started talking first. "Look, Luc will have our heads if we lose you and something happens. Please, just let us drive you to wherever you need to go, then we'll disappear until you need to go somewhere else. You won't even see us until then. And if you decide to walk, that's fine, but know we'll be tailing behind just to make sure you're okay. That's it. There'll be no dictating where you can and cannot go, or how long you stay or what you do there."

I eyed them. Surprisingly, Becca agreed with them. She pulled me aside and whispered, "I know I just saved you from Luc's place, and I know they remind you of Rich and his gang, but I also know Brandon. These are his people, and they take care of each other. I trust him, and as Luc is his brother, I trust Luc too."

"Becca—"

"And I know I'm being hypocritical about you being under someone's watch again, but I'm scared, and I know you are too. I can't believe I left the party and you ended up—" Becca started crying, and I wrapped her in my arms and cried with her. It had only been a month since I'd left Rich, and things kept changing back and forth from feeling safe to getting hurt. When was it going to end?

I turned to Damon and Brent and nodded my assent. Without a word, Damon turned to get the car while Brent came to stand near us, keeping us safe from the monster of an ex-boyfriend that wouldn't go away.

They drove me to the florist, and Ray ran over to me as soon as she saw me.

It was then I realized I was still in my torn dress under my coat. "Ray, do you still have the change of clothes you keep in the back?"

"Of course! What in the world happened?"

Becca stepped in and said, "Jill, why don't you go change? I'll catch Ray up."

"Okay." I nodded and headed out to the back where there was a shower and some clean clothes. Ray had installed it in her store many years ago when she started running. She said she loved running in the morning but could never wake up early enough, so this allowed her to get to work on time while also fitting in something she loved. I was thankful she'd had the foresight to put it in.

After a quick shower, I headed out to the front of the shop again to find Becca now had a cup of coffee in one hand. I saw another one steaming away on the counter.

"Here you go, sweetheart, this one's for you," Ray said, handing me the hot cup of goodness.

"Thank you." I took a long sip from the cup and didn't care that it was burning my throat all the way down.

I looked over the rim of my cup to see Becca and Ray staring at me. "I'm totally fine," I said firmly, then I pointed at Ray. "Don't even think about telling me to go home. I'm not going anywhere. I need this. I need the distraction."

Becca and Ray exchanged looks, and I didn't let out my breath until I saw Becca sigh. "Fine," she said. "But I'm going to stay here with you today. I already took the day off, so there's nowhere else I need to be."

I closed my mouth and smiled. "Well, let's get to work. What big party needs floral arrangements done today?"

Ray took the cue and went behind the counter to pull out the planning binder. We set to work right after, and I spent the rest of the day chatting with my two friends while putting together beautiful arrangements for other peoples' happily ever afters.

"You doing okay?" Becca asked, handing me a glass of wine.

Becca had insisted that she stay with me for the week. I

didn't argue with her because I felt better with someone near me, and I'd take her over the burly men Luc had following me any day.

"I'm doing fine." I held up the wine in thanks. "This helps."

"Jill, I—"

"You do not need to say sorry again. I'm okay," I said firmly. "You're here with me when I need you, which is now."

I was sinking lower into the sofa with each sip and could feel my eyes drooping, but then Becca said the one name that would wake me up. "So, Luc seems smitten with you."

"What?" I said, jackknifing upright. I laughed. "He's probably the least smitten with me out of anyone I know." Then I paused, remembering how Becca collected me from his room today. "You stormed in and got mad at him too, remember? Now you're defending him? What makes you think that he's smitten with me?"

"Brandon was saying—"

"I think you and Brandon are smitten," I said, cutting her off. "Where did *you* head off to last night, anyway?"

"Brandon was hungry, so we went out to eat. Work kept calling us, so we turned off our phones." She looked down when she said this, and I smiled.

"There was more, wasn't there?" I asked, stretching my leg out to give her a nudge.

Her head snapped up. "No, there wasn't. There's nothing going on there." She stood up abruptly and marched into the kitchen to refill her glass.

I got up to follow. "I'm sorry, I just don't get it. You two seem to be made for each other."

"You'd think, but I've tried, and he refuses to go past friendship. I think there's something wrong with me."

"There is definitely nothing wrong with you!"

"Well, tell that to him." She shook her head before I could

get another word in. "But we were not talking about me." She waggled a finger at me. "You're a sly one changing the subject like that."

I smirked and walked back to the couch. "I am not ready to be with another boy, even if you say he's a good guy. Plus, Luc stood me up last night and then tried to lock me up."

"Okay, yes, the locking up part is definitely troublesome. But he didn't stop you from leaving in the end, and he changed his mind about the ball and came looking for you. I see how you look at him too—all smoldering eyes like you can't get enough of him."

"I do not!"

"You so do." She smiled.

I was about to throw a pillow at her when we both smelled the smoke at the same time.

"The chicken!" we both yelled. Just like old times, neither one of us could cook.

LUC

"Sulking doesn't look good on you," Brandon said, sitting at my kitchen counter with a chicken leg in his hand.

"I don't understand why I can't go out with him to hunt this parasite down!" I growled.

"You know it's because we would all tear the guy limb from limb if we saw him first," Jacob said, taking a big bite out of a fried chicken leg.

"I would not." Brandon cocked an eyebrow at me, and I added, "I would bring him back and torture him slowly before tearing him apart limb from limb."

"Exactly," Brandon said.

"Well, why doesn't Mom let us? She's just as mad as we are at Pac hurting Sandy!" Bruno said. He was the youngest of us all and remembered the least about what had happened to our sister, but after all the stories we had told, he felt like he knew what had happened. Sandy also basically raised him, so he felt super protective of her.

"And why does it take this long?" I said, standing up and pacing. "I would have already found the guy if Dad had just let me go."

"Dredge is the best scout Dad has, and the others in the pack listen to him. Sit down and eat some food. And stop pacing, you're driving me crazy," Jacob said.

"I'm driving you crazy?" I whirled on him.

Brandon immediately came between us. He was the calmer sibling and the most like Mom. He stuck a chicken leg in my mouth, and I bit a big chunk out of it before plopping myself down on the sofa unceremoniously. All this waiting was going to drive me crazy, much less having my other brothers here doing the same.

"We're all wound up and know exactly how you feel, but Dad gave orders, and we have to stay put until we hear otherwise," Brandon said firmly.

I growled in response but continued to gnaw at the chicken leg.

Seeing that I was a bit calmer, Bruno ventured to ask, "Remind me again why Dad wants him alive?"

Brandon answered, which I was thankful for because I was so mad we hadn't heard anything from Dredge yet: "Pac saved Dad's life once."

"Sandy fell in love with him, didn't she?" Bruno asked.

"So hard. She thought he was her mate," Jacob said.

"Until he tried to pawn her off to another pack," I spit out. I still couldn't believe Dad had banished Pac instead of killing him. Now look at the problem we were in!

A pounding at the door made us all jump on full alert. I marched over and swung the door open.

Dredge stumbled in. "Hey, Luc, do you have any water?" he gasped out.

I signaled Bruno to grab some water and followed Dredge to the sofa. "Well, did you get him?"

"We did. All is well. I escorted him back to the pack, and he's under lock and key until further notice. I told Dad I'd come tell you personally so you could hear it from me and not someone else."

"What do you mean until further notice?" I growled, ignoring the rest of what he said. "He should have been taken care of immediately."

"You know why," said Dredge, giving me a glare over his cup. Dredge was older than all of us. Dad found him and Mom one night while trying to find his place in life. They'd been skin and bones. Dad immediately fell for Mom and took Dredge in as one of his own. He was the best big brother any of us could have asked for.

"How can you be so calm when it's Pac?" I yelled, wanting to punch him for even agreeing with Dad to bring in Pac intact.

"Because I know what's at stake." Dredge stood up and towered over me. "You know as well as I do that Pac escaped us once before. Now that we've finally found him, Dad wants to know why he was betrayed after everything he did for him. And you know Dad, he won't let it go."

"Tell us how you found him," Bruno said, sitting down on the other chair as though getting ready for a story.

I groaned, but everyone ignored me, so I plopped down on a stool at the kitchen counter.

"It was easy," Dredge began. "We waited in the hospital parking lot until we smelled him coming out." He looked over at me. "He really looks different. Totally would have fooled me except for his scent, but there is no mistaking that smell."

"Like following a basket full of potpourri, no?" Jacob said.

We all howled with laughter. It was always the running joke amongst us brothers that Pac smelled like he had bathed in a pond full of gardenias and autumn spices.

"Anyways," Dredge said, always the first to sober up. "We followed him to the building downtown that Jacob had followed him to and ambushed him before he could get in the building. He clearly did not want to make a scene, so he followed us to our car, and we escorted him to Dad. Easy peasy, and everyone stayed alive and unhurt."

"I smelled multiple wolves near or in his building. You didn't encounter anyone else?" Jacob said.

"Nope, just him. I smelled them, too, and we were on high alert, but no one else jumped out at us or tried to save him."

"He came calmly?" I asked skeptically. Pac was not known to be calm.

"He did." Dredge gave me a stern look. "I know who I smelled, Luc. My nose isn't damaged or anything."

"Of course not." I held up my hands in surrender. "I would never imply such a thing."

"Good." He gave me another stern look and went back to nursing his drink.

Dredge ended up staying for dinner, then left with Jacob and Bruno.

"You don't seem content," Brandon said when we were alone.

"Something isn't sitting well, but Dredge said he caught him, so I'm relieved. Pac's off the streets at least."

"What are you going to do about Jill?"

I was silent for a moment, contemplating what I was going to tell Brandon, but he beat me to it.

"I know you're into her," he said, giving me a nudge.

"I'm pretty sure I've scared her off."

"You won't know until you ask."

"What? Just go visit her with some flowers and ask for a do-over?" I laughed, wondering what fruit punch Brandon had been drinking.

"Hey, you said it yourself, you found your mate. You

weren't like this with Kit. I should know, I had to watch that train wreck."

This time I punched him hard. There was no reason for him to bring that up again. But he had a point. It couldn't hurt to try. My wolf had been upset all day. I thought he'd be better after knowing Pac was captured, but the calm that came over me after deciding to go chase after Jill was something else. Maybe I'd go pay her a visit tomorrow.

JILL

THE NEXT DAY I insisted Becca not join me at work; I was going to be just fine. After Brandon shared the news that Rich had been captured and he was no longer a problem, the relief that ran through me was exhilarating. I felt freer than I had ever felt before and would never take my freedom for granted again.

However, at work, Ray refused to let me do the big order of the day—six dozen roses of all shades and colors, liberally sprinkled with lilies and lavender. Instead, I watched Ray throughout the day as she picked, trimmed, and potted and wished that someone would give me flowers like that. One day, maybe that would happen.

On my way home, Ray asked me to drop off a couple of orders that the delivery guy wasn't able to pick up because he was busy on the big order run. The first was to a grandmother from her granddaughter for her birthday. I even sang her "Happy Birthday," which made her day. The other was to a mom of four, who was also celebrating a birthday. The husband and kids all crowded around her as we sang "Happy Birthday" to her. I felt so special to be included in these moments that I could see myself working in this floral business for longer than just a step to the next journey in my life.

When I got home, I pulled out my key, but Becca opened the door as soon as my key touched the keyhole.

"Look what you got!" She opened the door wide, and my eyes almost popped out of their sockets. Inside were six dozen roses of all shades and colors. The smell alone was intoxicating.

I gasped. "What?"

"That's what I'm wondering too. There's a card with it. I didn't open it, but here you go." She handed me a little envelope just like the ones Ray had at the store. Opening it up, Ray's handwriting jumped out at me.

Jill,

I know we didn't get off on the greatest footing, and I take full responsibility for that, but I would really like to get to know you and was hoping you would accept my sincerest apology and have dinner with me tonight.

Luc

He had signed his number under his name, and I stared at the card until Becca gave me a hug so tight I almost couldn't breathe.

"I knew it! He likes you!" she announced.

"I told you, Becca," I said, handing the card to her, "I'm not interested in being with a guy right now and he stood me up quite grandly the last time. And if you forgot, he kept me under house arrest yesterday."

"Yes, I do remember that." She sighed. "Do you want me to call him? I can let him down easy."

"Please do."

I went to the kitchen while Becca made the call. Thankfully, she walked to the bedroom so I couldn't hear the conversation. I wiped a tear from my eye. The yearning I felt for Luc was not gone, but I really wasn't ready. It was too soon after Rich.

The next day, Ray handed me a letter with someone else's handwriting on it and one rose.

Jill,

I know I did you wrong by not going with you to the ball. I own that mistake, and I wish I could do it over. I would dance with you all night. I could have prevented what happened, and I will never forgive myself for not being there for you.

I feel a strong connection with you. I will beg, if needed, for a chance to take you out again. This time it won't be just for ice cream, though. But if that's what you want, then I'm happy with that too.

Say yes, and let me take you to dinner tonight.

Luc

I slipped the note into my pocket and didn't say anything to Ray for the rest of the day, just took the order slips and made the flowers until it was time for me to go.

"Jill," Ray said on my way out, "you should know he hand-delivered the note to me this morning when I opened the shop."

I turned to look at Ray, feeling little goosebumps forming on my arms. "He did?"

"He was already here, waiting. He wanted to make sure you got it."

I looked down at my hand, which was hidden in my pocket and currently touching the note. Rich had been like this when he first met me, too, sending me love letters and wooing me by doing all the right things. How did I know if I could trust Luc?

"I know Luc. Grew up with him, you know. He was always the one helping out wherever he could. He's a good man."

"Oh . . ." I wasn't sure what I should say, though I could feel a bit of a crack in my resolve. "I'll think about it."

"Goodnight, Jill."

"Goodnight, Ray."

I held onto the note the entire walk home, wondering if I should call Luc and say yes. It was just a dinner after all. Nothing more.

"Did you call him last night?" Ray asked as soon as I set foot into the flower shop the next morning.

"No, I chickened out. He says he wants to get to know me and all these other nice things, but he doesn't know my past."

"Sweetie, your past does not define you. And Rich is gone, Luc said so himself. They took care of him."

"I know, but it's so soon, and I'm just getting my life together again."

"Well, don't get mad at me, but he was here again this morning."

"Again?" I was shocked Luc was being so persistent. Especially after getting denied by Becca's phone call and me ghosting him last night.

"Yeah." Ray pulled out a hat box from under the counter with another rose on top of it.

"Wow."

The box looked old. I opened the pink ribbon that was sewn on the sides of the box, careful to not pull on any loose strands as I peeled off the ribbon. I gasped when I pulled off the top lid. Inside the box was the black and red mask I'd fallen in love with at the masquerade ball. A note was tucked in the side, and I opened it.

Jill,

I saw you staring at this mask when I found you at the ball. You looked so content and happy I didn't want to disturb you. All the masks on the wall belong to my mom's side of the family. This particular one belonged to her. She had it made for the first masquerade ball she threw with my dad. It was the most exquisite mask of the time. I'd like you to have it. And I have a place for you to wear it if you'll have dinner with me tonight.

Luc

"Oh!" Ray had come up behind me and was reading the note over my shoulder.

"Privacy!" I exclaimed, stuffing the note into my pocket.

"Sorry, I couldn't help it. I'd been curious about what was in the box since he dropped it off this morning. That mask is absolutely gorgeous."

"Yeah, isn't it?" I ran my hand through the feathery fringes, thinking about what he said.

"What are you going to do?"

"I'm not sure. He's being so nice and persistent, and I *am* really drawn to him. But I'm scared, Ray."

She pulled me into a hug. "I would be more worried if you weren't scared."

"Really?" I mumbled into her shoulder. "You think I should go?"

"If nothing else, see if you've made a new friend. No one says you have to be romantic with him even if he wants to be with you. Take it slow."

"Okay, I'll think about it."

"Fantastic." Ray gently pulled away and looked at my face. "You cry as much as you want. Any time you like."

"Thanks, Ray. You've really allowed me to get a new life started again."

"Of course. Any friend of Becca's is a friend of mine."

I straightened my back, having had enough of my crying session. "Okay, now what project can I work on today?"

Ray, taking my cue, reached under the counter for the project binder. "Let's see. We have a wedding to finish preparing for today. Looks like flowers for the aisle are what's left."

"Then let's get started," I said, walking toward the back of the store to gather the supplies.

I worked in the back of the shop for the rest of the day while Ray fielded customers in the front. I had to keep redoing my bouquets because my mind was on Luc the whole time. After a while, a pile of torn ribbons and flowers was all I had to show for my work, and I sat down in frustration. My brain knew I shouldn't be doing this. I wasn't ready, but my heart was screaming at me to say yes.

I threw the bouquet I was working on onto the table. This was no use. Ray had already made six bouquets, even while fielding customers, and I was only on my second one.

I took out my phone and texted Luc's number with a simple "Yes." As soon as I sent it, my heart settled, and a comforting hum went through my body. Immediately, his response came back with a heart and a time and a location of where to meet, as well as a note to bring the mask with me. Curiosity overcame me, and I asked him for more details only to be told "All in good time."

LUC

"Don't you think this is a bit grand for a first date?" Jacob asked.

"No."

"No? Are you crazy? You're going to scare her off before she even gets to know you, and you haven't exactly made the best impression so far," Bruno said.

"Why are you two here? I thought you went home with Dredge," I snapped back.

"Brandon said you got a date, and we had to come and see you get all dressed up," Jacob said.

"And goad you as well. We're never too far away that we can't come and do that," Bruno added.

I gave them a glare and wished Brandon was here. He, at least, might have some input on if what I was wearing was too much, whereas these two hooligans couldn't put on a decent pair of pants between them.

I added the finishing touches to my tie and turned to look at my younger brothers. "It's not a first date as we've already had one."

"You did?" Jacob asked.

"How come we're just hearing about this?" Bruno was now standing in front of me with an expectant look.

"Well? Are you going to tell us more?" Jacob insisted.

"No, except that it involved ice cream."

"Really? That's it? Ice cream?" Bruno threw his arms up and walked back to the living room.

"Now you know her favorite dessert," I told them.

"Huh. You're so going to bomb tonight," Jacob said.

I reached out and took Jacob under my arm and ruffled his hair. He managed to wrap his arms around me and spin me onto my back.

"You're going to break me before I pick her up," I groaned.

"Nah, you're too hefty for that," Jacob said.

"Hefty?" I pumped my muscles for them to see. "I think I'm more fit than your blubbery stomach," I said, swatting at Jacob's mid-section.

"Well, use those muscles to protect your girl, yeah?" Bruno said.

I took a good look at the two of them and eyed them warily. "You two worried about something?"

"No," they both said, a bit too quickly.

"No?" I glared at them, knowing that if I stood my ground long enough one of them would break.

Sure enough, Bruno said, "Just something we heard Dredge say on the way up."

Jacob punched him in the side.

"Hey! He deserves to know," Bruno returned. "This is his mate after all."

"You agree Jill is my mate?" I asked them.

Bruno nodded. "We've never seen you all worked up about a girl like this before. Not even Kit. And we like Jill."

I gave a nod, acknowledging their love. "What's this about what Dredge said?"

"There was another scent that smelled the same as Pac when they were at the building, but it was coming from a different direction. They ignored it, but Dredge thought it was odd," Bruno said, but they both looked serious.

I put a hand on their shoulders, giving them a squeeze. "I'm sure it was just the wind or something carrying his smell in a different direction. I'll take care of Jill, don't worry."

JILL

HE TOLD me to meet him on the corner of Main and Wilcox. There wasn't anything special here except the general store and the library. I hadn't gone exploring at the library yet, but on taking a good look at it for the first time since arriving in this town, it was a lot bigger than I thought. I was excited to go in and see if I could find some good reads there one day. I logged it in the back of my mind when I saw Luc coming toward me from across the street.

My heart raced seeing him all dressed up. He looked exactly like what I thought he'd look like the night of the masquerade ball.

He had a simple black mask in his hand, and I wondered where we could possibly be going. Becca had lent me a simple, strapless, black dress that really made my headdress stand out. I had also borrowed her three-inch red pumps, which made me almost the same height as Luc.

"Thank you for joining me tonight," he said, his husky voice stirring feelings inside of me I thought had gone dormant. "You look gorgeous."

"You look good yourself." Was that the best I could do?

He had me all tongue-tied he looked so good. "Where are we going?"

"First up," he said, taking my hand and resting it on his arm, "is dinner."

"Here?" I asked, looking at the general store and then the library.

He laughed. "No. But behind the library is a little Taiwanese shop that is owned by a woman I've known forever. She makes the best Taiwanese food in the world."

"That sounds delicious," I said, genuinely happy.

He led me behind the library and, sure enough, a door with an awning and a couple of small plants at the entrance invited us into a well-lit room with seats for six. We were greeted by an older lady who looked to be in her seventies. Her hair was a beautiful soft white, and she had the kindest black eyes.

"Luc, so good to see you," she announced in a charming soft voice.

"Bubbie, this is Jill."

"Ah, Luc told me about you."

I was startled that she knew about me since Luc and I hardly knew each other, but she exuded warmth just like Miti, and I relaxed in her presence. Come to think of it, I hadn't seen Miti in a while. I made a note to ask Luc about Miti later.

Luc led me to one of the seats. "This looks like a private home with seating for a family," I said.

"It is. Bubbie used to have a restaurant. She seated about eighty people, and everyone in town knew her, but about ten years ago she decided she'd had enough, closed the shop, and opened up this place in her home. She leased the front of the house to the city so that a library could be put in, but the kitchen and a connecting room with a bathroom are all hers."

"Wow, I feel so special," I said, and I meant it. This was not what I had expected from tonight. After the big show of flowers, I had thought Luc would bring me to a ritzy place where he'd show off how much money he had and try to dazzle me like Rich had done.

"As you should," Luc said, shaking out his napkin and placing it on his lap.

He let his hand drop right next to mine, and his thumb found its way to the top of my hand, rubbing it gently. I willed myself to not jolt away and startle him. I kept telling myself that the warmth shooting up my arm was what I was supposed to feel, but I still had to duck my head down because I could feel droplets forming in the corner of my eyes. A man hadn't touched me like this in a really long time.

"What's wrong?" Luc had scooted around and was now sitting next to me with an arm on the back of my seat.

"Oh." I looked up, wiping the tears from my eyes. "It's nothing—nothing you're doing, at least. I mean, it is, but it's not. Oh, sorry, let me start over."

He laughed, pulling me in for a hug. "You're safe with me. Rich is gone, and you're safe, I promise."

The feel of his strong muscles around me made me tense for a second, reminding me of Rich's 'protective' hugs when other men were around. I could tell he felt it, too, as his arms started loosening around me. I let them loosen, unsure of the feelings I was having, and we separated, looking at each other.

His eyes were smoldering, and I could tell he wanted more from me, which scared me, but I felt myself flush under his gaze. It was infuriating to experience the feelings that were coursing through me. I wanted him, but I was too scared to reach out and touch him. What if he was the same as Rich? I couldn't survive another downward spiral.

Thankfully, Bubbie came out right then with two hot bowls ladled with food.

I looked at Luc and whispered, "We didn't order."

"No one orders here. You just sit and Bubbie feeds you."

"Oh." A smile crept across my face. I loved this.

"You two lovebirds; so sweet," Bubbie said, looking at Luc and then me with the most loving eyes.

I focused my eyes on the food in front of us and breathed in a big whiff of the delicious smell. I really teared up this time. "This is amazing," I said, looking up at Bubbie. "I haven't had this in so long."

A big smile crossed her face, and she nodded. "Luc said you might be missing some homecooked Taiwanese meals, so I made a big pot of beef noodle soup. It is my specialty."

I was already picking up my chopsticks, and with my soup spoon in my other hand, I leaned in for my first bite. I heard Luc chuckle next to me, but that was the last I heard as the food was all-consuming.

When I finally came up to breathe, I saw Luc had already finished his meal and was talking with Bubbie off to the side. They looked so comfortable together, like grandmother and grandson. And the more I stared at them, the more I thought that might be true. I was about to ask them if they were when they both turned to me.

"You seemed to enjoy it," Bubbie said, coming over to pick up my bowl.

"It was absolutely delicious. Reminded me of my mom's." This seemed to please her and made me smile. "I can get these," I added. Standing, I picked up our dishes and asked her to direct the way.

She succumbed and showed me to the back where her kitchen was. It was immaculate, even though I knew how much time and mess it took to make this meal. Or maybe it was just me, as I tended to be messy in the kitchen.

"I love your kitchen." I turned in small circles, admiring all its nooks and crannies. There were a number of recipe books, a huge island where I could see myself baking, and an array of cabinets that had my imagination starting to fill them with mixers, baking supplies, pots, and pans.

"Jill, come see this," Luc said from the left.

I turned to see him opening what looked like a regular cabinet door, only to reveal a whole other room behind it! My jaw dropped. This was amazing!

Luc beckoned. "There's more."

That comment was the only reason I moved; I was too dumbstruck to do anything more.

Inside the room was yet another door that opened into a huge pantry. It was filled to the brim with food and baking supplies, as well as gadgets galore.

"Would you like to come back and help me with meals from time to time?" Bubbie asked, coming up behind us.

"Yes!" I said without thinking. "This would be a dream come true. I love cooking and baking, and I cannot believe the space you have here. You have your own industrial kitchen."

"I did once own a restaurant. It's what I'm used to."

I blushed, remembering that now. Of course, she would require a space where she could have full access to what she used to have.

"But not today," Luc said, putting a hand on the small of my back and ushering us out of the kitchen. We were outside again, saying bye to Bubbie before I could think about what was happening.

"Hey, I wanted to stay there for a bit longer," I protested.

He smiled down at me. "And you can come back whenever you'd like—except for right this second, because I have a surprise for you."

"Oh."

He bent down to kiss the top of my head, and it sent shivers down my back. My hand fit neatly into his as he guided me back to the front of the library and across the street to some iron gates that led into a dark alley.

I immediately let go of his hand, halting.

"It's okay. It's not what you think," he assured me.

"I'd rather not, Luc." I looked at him, and I could tell he was confused as to why I wasn't following him.

"Does this have to do with Rich? We haven't really talked about it—"

"It does, and . . . I'm just not sure. This alley is bringing up too many bad memories."

All of a sudden, Luc grabbed me and pulled me toward him. A moment later, I heard the sound of someone falling and skidding across the sidewalk. We both turned our heads to look back and saw three teenage kids with their skateboards running away.

"You okay?" he whispered into my hair. He was holding me so tight I almost couldn't breathe. "I heard them coming and one of them lost control. They almost knocked into you."

"I'm fine. Thank you."

He didn't let me go but loosened his hold enough so I could look up into his face. His fingers found the loose strands in front of my ear and tucked them behind the shell ever so gently that I only felt the slight tips of his fingers grazing my skin. "I'm not going to let anything happen to you, Jill. I promise. I'm going to keep telling you that until you believe me. We don't have to use this alley. They have another entrance, but I would love it if you'd come with me tonight to see this surprise. I think you'll really like it, and I'm hoping to make up for missing the ball the other day."

"Hence the masks," I whispered. I was so enthralled by how close we were that I could hardly breathe. I already knew it was going to be a long night of second-guessing myself if I didn't say yes.

"I swear on Becca and Brandon that you are safe with me," Luc now added firmly.

Becca was definitely someone I could trust, and Brandon, too, as far as Becca was concerned. "Okay, show me."

A wide grin spread across his face, and he looked even more handsome than before. It was contagious, and I found myself smiling back at him as he led me around the building to the main entrance.

It was the local theatre, and the man in the ticket booth was wearing suspenders and a straw hat, smiling at us like we were coming to buy tickets to a movie. Why couldn't we have just come to the entrance to begin with?

"Hi, Luc."

I sent Luc a smirk. "Do you know everyone in this town?"

"Yes."

"Oh." I didn't know what else to say. There wasn't a chance I knew all the people in my schools while growing up, much less the whole town or city.

Luc had shown the guy a couple of tickets, and we were met by someone dressed in a brown suit, who looked over our attire and ushered us in.

"Put on your mask," Luc whispered to me.

He helped tie the ribbon on the back, then took my hand and tucked it into the crook of his arm before leading me into the entrance. He guided me to the right, where a set of plush, carpeted stairs led into a well-lit hallway. We passed by the token bathrooms, ones where there would have been a line up the stairs to the entrance if there was a live show going on.

At the other end of the hallway was another set of doors. A man dressed from the twenties opened the door, and what greeted us in the open-air room was not what I expected. People in period clothes were walking around, dressed in both simple and extravagant dresses with matching masks. They were carrying cocktails and talking in whispers.

Luc leaned down to my ear and said, "Welcome to our Speakeasy."

"An actual Speakeasy?" I gasped, not realizing these things existed anymore. I'd only ever read about these in books; a hidden place that served illegal alcohol during prohibition.

"Yes, but more for fun nowadays. Come on, I'll get you a drink."

"Oh, I don't drink," I said, only half paying attention. There was so much to see. I hadn't even finished looking at the beautiful setting around me, much less begun people-watching.

"You do drink water, though, right?"

I looked at Luc and saw him smiling at his own joke. "Yes," I said, smiling along with him. "Bubbly, please."

I followed Luc through what looked like a gambling room to a den where people were sitting, talking, and playing darts. A small bar sat in the corner. He guided me through a set of double doors next, which led to a much longer bar. The people behind the counter were dressed in period clothing too. I loved it!

Luc got our drinks, and he led me back to the main area where I noticed the stage curtains had opened and someone was performing. At this point, an usher came up and escorted us to some seats at the very front.

I had never experienced anything like this before. For all intents and purposes, it felt as though we'd been whisked back to the 1920s. I had my mask on so no one would know it was me, but this time Luc was by my side. I could feel him looking at me from time to time, and I loved the warmth his attention created. After the performance, which had been an entertaining mix of singing and joking, we got up to explore the building further after overhearing there were more rooms to discover.

One room was a changing room, and we were able to see the actors and actresses putting on makeup, discussing their scripts, and going about their business. Then there was a room filled with sofas and comfy chairs. Two men were in there doing impromptu dances and singing a few songs with a couple of the guests. It was entertaining, and I was having the time of my life!

Many of the rooms were dimmed, and soft music played everywhere we went. It provided a calming backdrop behind the quiet murmur of conversations filling the air that I found myself relaxing.

We sat down back in the room with the bar and dart boards and enjoyed some private time in the corner. Our masks were in our laps, and I'd been comfortably nudged into the crook of Luc's arm, my head resting on his shoulder.

"The man with the face like a clown was hilarious, wasn't he?" I said.

"The mime?"

"Yeah, him." I sighed with contentment. "All the actors have been so good. I feel like we've been whisked back to the twenties, and I don't want to leave."

"I could bring you again."

He seemed to hold his breath for a second, and I lifted my head off his chest to look him in the eye. I smiled. "I'd like that."

His eyes warmed. "Bubbie really liked you," he now said quietly.

"I really liked her as well," I admitted.

"She's my mom's mom."

"Your grandmother? Why didn't you say so?"

"Forgive me, but I wanted to see how you two got along first. Bubbie likes her privacy the older she gets, and the last time I introduced her to a girl she got really attached. I think it broke her heart a bit when she left me."

"I'm sorry," I said.

He blinked. "You're not mad at me?"

"Why would I be mad at you?"

"Because we're on a date, and I took you to her restaurant."

I sat up to look at him properly. "I'm confused. Because we're on a date, you'd think I'd be mad at you for not introducing the lady who cooked us dinner as your grandmother?"

I watched as he released a big ball of air. "Yeah, I was worried about exactly that."

"Don't be silly. We hardly know each other ourselves."

I went back to snuggling into his side and commenced watching the shenanigans happening at the bar. We were quiet for a bit until Luc whispered into my ear, "What happened that night at the ball?"

I knew he would ask at some point, and I'd thought I wouldn't tell him or anyone about it. I had also been very angry with him and how he'd treated me the following day. But tonight had been magical, and I felt safe in his arms. Luc provided me with a sense of security I hadn't felt in a long time.

"You said you saw me at the mask museum," I began quietly.

"Yes." His arm tightened around my back in silent encouragement to continue.

"I was asked for a dance, and I said yes."

"I saw that too."

I paused, digesting that little tidbit. "I ended up dancing quite a bit after that."

"I saw your other dances too."

"Oh—"

"And was stupid enough to not ask you for one of those dances," he said sharply, his tone self-derisive.

"I would have really liked that," I confessed, squeezing his arm.

He gave me a squeeze in return and planted a soft kiss on my head in reply.

"I was drunk on happiness and freedom that I wasn't thinking when I followed my first dance partner upstairs," I continued, feeling my heart begin to pound with the memory of that moment. "He led me into an empty room."

"He didn't do anything to you, did he?" Luc was instantly on high alert. I could also hear him breathing fast, and a low rumbling sound was coming from his chest.

I rubbed his shoulders and looked him in the eye, trying to soothe him. I was afraid he might explode. "No. No, he didn't do anything. It was just Rich's goon leading me to Rich," I assured him. Maybe I shouldn't be telling him any more about Rich?

"But he did something," Luc seethed.

"No! Luc, it's okay. I mean, he tried, but a group of people came into the room just in time and I was able to escape. I ran and fell down the stairs. That's where I got most of my bruises and cuts. Rich didn't hit me, though." Surprisingly enough, it was the one time he hadn't managed to get his fists on me.

"What did he do to you before when you were with him?" Luc asked in a low, controlled voice. If it wasn't so dim in here with candlelight dancing around the room, I would have sworn his eyes had just glowed.

"Why do you ask?" I whispered.

"You're shaking, and you do that every time you mention Rich. I want to know who hurt my mate."

"Your mate?" *Did I hear that right?*

Seeming to realize what he'd said, he changed directions. "I care about the people around me. We recently found out Rich is the same person that hurt my sister many years ago."

"You have a sister?"

"Yes, she's the oldest sibling."

"And Rich hurt her?"

"His name was Pac back then."

I started shaking even more and felt cold all of a sudden.

Luc noticed. He took off his jacket and put it around my shoulders. "I'm sorry," he murmured. "We don't need to talk about him anymore. I'm sorry for bringing him up right now, especially when we were having such a wonderful evening."

"No, it's okay. I knew I would have to tell you at some point. It's just . . . the thought of him hurting another woman makes me sick to my stomach."

"Okay, that's enough," he said firmly.

I turned to face him. "What about you?"

"What about me?" he asked, a brow lifted.

"Do you have a girlfriend story?"

His muscles tensed, and I wondered what his story was, but he only said, "No."

My instinct was to push further, but I reminded myself it was our first date, and we'd just tried to go through my story already. We could save his one for another night.

"Okay, shall we go dance?" I asked him instead. "I remember passing a room that had louder music."

"Sounds good." He got up and held out his hand. I took it and followed him out of the bar.

JILL

My bed was rocking. I peeled one lid open and saw Becca lying next to me with an expectant look on her face.

"Good morning to you too," I mumbled, and I went to roll over and go hide under the covers.

"Oh no, you don't!" Becca exclaimed. "Spill! How was your night?"

"Let me get some more sleep first."

"It's almost nine, and you're going to be late for work."

"Oh my goodness!" I sat up immediately and saw the clock said seven. "It's not that soon!"

"But now you're awake and can tell me all about your night."

"Like I'm going to tell you now," I grumbled.

"Jill, please. My love life is in shambles. Please let me live through yours."

I turned to glare at her and said, "It was fun, and you were right. Luc is a fantastic guy."

"I knew it! No brother of Brandon's could be bad."

"No." I sat up straight as I began to remember our night. "I met his grandmother, Becca, and she's Taiwanese," I said, feeling my eyes widen. I wanted her to know how significant that was.

"He introduced you to his grandmother already? And she's Asian?"

"Yeah!"

Becca sat there looking flummoxed, and I went over and nudged her. "You okay?"

"Huh? Oh yeah, I am," she whispered. "Brandon has never mentioned his grandparents to me before, or that he's of mixed heritage. I always just assumed he was white."

"If he never told you, you would never know. There's nothing you could have found out."

"Yeah, I know. I just wish he did."

"Oh, Becca! You'll find your Prince Charming someday. He's out there, I'm sure of it. For someone as good as you, I'd be surprised if he wasn't right around the corner, and if Brandon can't deal with that and step up to the plate, then he's not worth it."

She looked so dejected that I gave her a big hug. Becca had done so much for me; I hated seeing her miserable. "And it's not like I've found my Prince Charming, either," I added. "Luc and I have only gone out on one official date."

She gave me a big eye roll.

"It's been one date!" I said again firmly.

"You should see the way he looks at you, Jill. I'm wondering why he hasn't already proposed."

I felt my face flush. "Oh, be quiet. Look, I have to get ready for work."

Becca laughed. She jumped out of my bed and gave me a quick salute as she left the room. The whole time, all I could think about was Luc; how he'd smelled and felt last night. We'd ended up dancing the night away, not coming home till well after midnight.

It was a cold, foggy day with some light rain the next morning. Becca had offered to drive me to work on her way back into the city, but I was so distracted with my thoughts that I couldn't get ready in time. Plus, a little rain and cold never hurt anyone, so I told her I would walk.

There were usually people bustling around from store to store in town or just sauntering through on their morning walk, but this morning it was quiet. Everyone appeared to be staying indoors, and I was okay with that. I felt like I had the whole world to myself as I daydreamed about my night out with Luc.

I basked in the warm feelings the memories elicited. I hadn't had so much fun in a long time, not to mention that I'd got to eat beef noodle soup. That was something I hadn't eaten since Mom passed away, and I'd almost forgotten what it tasted like.

I was jumping over a puddle when a black car pulled up next to me. I didn't think anything of it until I saw a familiar face exit the back seat. Before I could scream, something was slapped over my mouth, and the next thing I knew it was pitch black and consciousness fled.

I woke up to darkness and the smell of rotten sewage. I could hear voices in the background, the sound of groaning somewhere near me, and the scuttling of what sounded like rats. A dim light in the distance provided some hope to the oppressive darkness. I reached out in front of me, testing my surroundings, but all I felt was empty air. I moved forward slowly, inching my feet forward one step at a time. My heart was pounding in my chest, and I felt lightheaded. No, this couldn't be happening. This was all a dream, right? It had to be. Just a really, really bad dream that I was going to wake up from at any moment. That explained why I could feel nothing in front of me—I was dreaming.

But then my fingers hit what felt like a metal bar. I reached out further, only to find another metal bar two inches from the next metal bar, and the next, and the next . . .

Something hit the bar, which made me startle, and a pain shot through my ankle at the same moment. The sprain from the masquerade ball was still there and seemed worse.

"Sweetheart," a voice drawled from the other side of the bar. A lamp turned on, and I saw two burly men sitting at a card table, staring right at me not more than ten feet away. "You remember us?"

My heart rate skyrocketed when I saw who they were. "Please, don't do this. You don't have to listen to him. Let me go. I'm nothing to any of you."

"That's not what the boss said. He said you broke his heart when you left. Left a big crater in his chest that he doesn't know how to fill. He feels betrayed," the second guy said.

I swallowed, searching for the right words to persuade him. "Dwayne, right? You're the one who lifted me up when I fell that time getting out of the car? Thank you for that. It proved to me that you're not like Rich. You don't have to be like him, either. You can let me go and come with me. Start your life over again."

Dwayne looked at the man next to him, and there was silence for a second where I hoped—not a lot, but just a smidge—that they would let me out. But that was quickly shattered when the first guy grabbed something off the table and threw it at the bars. It hit with a loud clang before clattering across the floor. They burst into raucous laughter, smacking the table as if they were half-drunk.

I saw that it was a cooked rib bone. How dare they! I shuddered at the thought that they had just been eating and were throwing their food at me.

A groan came from behind me again, and Dwayne noticed it this time too. He lifted the lamp toward the sound, and I turned to see it was another person huddled in a ball, rocking themselves back and forth in the corner.

"Be quiet, old woman!" Dwayne growled. "You've been groaning up a storm since you got here. If you'd eat the food we gave you, maybe you'd feel better."

Another round of raucous laughter ensued, and I imagined they had provided no food for the woman—or they had eaten the food meant for her. I wondered how long she'd been here.

The light dimmed down, and the men continued doing whatever they were doing in the glow of the lamp.

I began shuffling to the woman as soon as they looked away. Something about her felt familiar. Her rocking and groaning guided me forward until I felt the cloth of her dress in my hand.

I screamed as a hand wrapped itself around mine, holding me tight. A couple of rib bones hit the bars again, along with shouts of "Quiet down!"

I willed my heart rate to slow down and kept telling myself it was just an old lady.

"Are you okay?" I whispered, hoping the guards were hard of hearing and would leave us alone for a bit. I leaned forward when she mumbled something. It was hard to catch what she was saying as she kept rocking and speaking barely above a whisper.

I leaned closer until I was sitting right next to her and heard, "I need to change. I need to change. It's the only way. The only way. Must save family. Family in danger." Then she'd repeat the mantra again. A closer look at her made me startle. This old lady wasn't just anyone—it was Miti!

"Miti!" I whispered. "How are you here?"

But she couldn't or wouldn't respond to me. She just kept rocking and repeating herself. I lay down where I was and cried at our fate.

LUC

"Bʀᴏ, ʏᴏᴜ ʟᴏᴏᴋ ɢᴏᴏᴅ," Jacob said.

"Why are you still here?" I asked, pulling my t-shirt over my head. It was the fifth one I'd tried on, and if not for Jacob, I might have tried on more. But in order to get him to shut his mouth I needed to pick something, so I settled on the solid blue shirt I had just put on.

After last night, I was extra nervous about making a good impression on Jill. Last night was the best night I'd had in a long time. She was my one and only, and I didn't want to scare her off; there would be nowhere for me to go except after her.

"You're really going to surprise her?" Jacob asked.

"Why not? It's just lunch, and we're not going far. Just to the diner down the street."

Jacob raised a brow. "You're taking her out to a diner on your second date?"

"She's very easygoing, not like you."

"Still, even I know a diner is not where you would take a date."

"Leave him alone," Brandon said, coming into my room. "The boy is in love; let him be."

"As if you aren't," I said, sending him a look. "When are you going to act on it?"

"You know I can't," he growled.

"Can't or won't?" Jacob said.

Before a fight could break out, I spritzed myself with some cologne and sprayed Brandon as well for the fun of it. He immediately gasped and forgot what he had been doing.

"I'm heading out. You all need to go home," I said, pointing at all my brothers.

"Yes, sir!" I heard from behind me as the door closed, but it was soon followed by their laughter.

"What do you mean she never came to work?" I bellowed.

Ray flinched, which I immediately was sorry for, but I couldn't control the temper growing inside me. My wolf wanted to be let out to run and find Jill. It needed to know she was safe.

"She never came in. And there's no need to yell."

I slammed my hand on the counter and sucked in a deep breath. She was right. Me fuming at her didn't solve anything. It was time I listened to my wolf and let it out to find her.

"She's probably at home. Maybe she got a bug or something," Ray continued. "I really think she's just fine."

I stared at Ray, then stormed out. She wasn't fine, and I knew it. Something wasn't right.

I retraced the steps she would have taken from her home and stopped when a sweet smell hit my nose. Pac! Why was his smell here? I immediately darted for the trees and transformed before I was fully concealed. It was time to pay Pac a visit and see with my own eyes what in the world was going on.

I was halfway to Dad's territory when I heard howling from behind me. I stopped to see Brandon and the others coming up from behind.

"Why are you headed to Dad's?" Brandon asked in my mind, coming to a stop in front of me and blocking my way.

"I've missed him," I replied sharply, swatting him with my paw.

"I don't believe that for one second," Jacob said, taking a nip at my ears.

"What do you guys want?" I was in a hurry, and every second was wasting time. I tried going around Brandon, but Jacob and Bruno surrounded me on either side.

"We heard you howling and thought we'd join you because if you're going home, it can't be good," Brandon said.

"Plus, Dad has been in a mood, and you might need some backup," Bruno said.

I looked at my brothers and vowed to see them more often. "Let's go then." We started running again and didn't slow down until we got to the border of Dad's territory.

"You sure you want to do this? You know what Dad's going to ask about," Brandon said.

I swung my head to look at him. "I have to. Something's very wrong, and I know it's to do with Pac."

"Let's go. I'm getting restless," Bruno said.

We ran until we saw Mom standing in front of us. She was clearly waiting for us to approach. I made the change back into my human form first, my brothers following suit.

"Luc, you know with you being here, your Dad will feel challenged," Mom said, staring me down.

"I'm not allowed to come home?" I growled.

"Not without a mate."

"This *is* about my mate!"

Mom's eyes immediately glowed, and a huge smile spread across her face. "You've found someone? Not Kit, I hope."

"No! It's a woman called Jill, and she's in trouble. I need to see Pac."

"Pac? He's here?" She looked at all of her sons, waiting on one of us to speak up. None of us dared. It was just like Dad to hide something like this under her nose.

Bruno never knew when to keep his mouth shut, though, because he said, "Dredge brought him back. We found him earlier this week."

Mom let out a growl that sent us groveling. She shifted and sped off. I shifted back and swatted at Bruno to let him know how much of a dunce he was. Now we'd all be in trouble.

We chased after Mom. I was hoping we hadn't done that much damage that I wouldn't be able to see Pac, but apparently, that was not going to be an issue.

Shifting back to human form before we entered our parents' home, we found Mom and Dad arguing, with Sandy looking on from the side. When she saw me, Sandy ran over and enveloped me in a huge hug. I hadn't seen my sister in over a year, and I had to say it was good to see her again.

"What are you doing back here?" she asked. "And why is Mom so upset and yelling about Pac? I thought he was taken care of a long time ago?"

She was visibly shaking, and I hated that all this history was being dug up again and affecting her.

Brandon came and put an arm around her, and Jacob stood on the other side. She knew she was in good hands with us, but I wondered why Dad had kept Pac a secret this whole time. Where was he keeping him?

I walked up to Dad slowly, who still hadn't seen me, and that was probably for the best. But when I got within a few feet of him, he looked right at me and said, "Don't move an inch more. I knew you were here as soon as you crossed my border. Do you have a mate yet?"

His eyes bored into me, and I could feel the intensity of his disappointment. Kit had really done a number on us all. Dad was ready to name me alpha when he thought Kit was the one. I had definitely treated her like my mate, so he'd been let down just as much as I had.

"I've found her. My mate, that is, not Kit."

"Then where is she?"

"She's in danger, and I need to speak with Pac."

"You too?" he roared. "You're the one who sent us on this wild goose chase to find him, and all we got was a dud!"

"A dud? What are you talking about?"

"It's not Pac, and now what am I supposed to do with a human as a prisoner?"

"A human?" all of us yelled at once.

"Yes. You played me for a fool, and I won't tolerate it."

"Dad, what are you talking about?" Brandon asked, standing between Dad and me. Brandon had always been the favorite, and I hoped that worked in our favor right now, because when Dad got riled up, it was not a good sign.

Dad let out a deep breath, and his shoulders sagged. He suddenly looked decades older than I remembered. A pain shot through me, thinking about all the time I had not spent with him. "You want to talk to him?" he asked us. "I'll let him explain it to you. Goodness knows I can't make heads or tails about it."

With a subdued air surrounding us all and the rest of the pack looking on, we followed Dad deep into the woods. A clearing had been made between a group of trees, and under some foliage was a makeshift housing. I could see the edge of a mattress sticking out of the entrance.

Two guards came forward at our approach but immediately backed down when they saw Dad.

"Bring him out," Dad ordered.

The would-be Pac was brought into the clearing, and I immediately growled. "That's not him! Not even close!"

"Yes, I already told you that!" Dad said.

"No, that's not the guy we saw at the hospital, I mean—not even a little bit!"

"What?" Dredge said, coming to join us. "It's definitely him. He got his face redone, but he smells exactly the same . . . "

We were all staring at Dredge now, because the way he trailed off and the way he was staring intently at Pac sent a current of alarm through the rest of us.

"Tell them what you told me," Dad said, standing to his full height and looking less than pleased at the situation. The rest of us copied his stance, and I could see the human shrinking right before our eyes. He was cowered so low to the ground that I felt sorry for him—until I remembered Jill. Then I stood even straighter, waiting impatiently for his reply.

"Tell them!" Dad roared.

The rest of us flinched but didn't budge.

He began to explain. At first, I couldn't believe what he was saying until I remembered that Jill had said Pac was a top-notch plastic surgeon who had a side project he was working on.

"I was a science project, one of the first," he continued. "But there were many after me. I really didn't see the harm in what he was doing. He just wanted us to all smell like him. Said it was for the scientific good; like a perfume, you know, but more permanent. He paid us well for it, and well, it was the money that really made me agree. I was able to buy a house and travel again. I've honestly never seen any of you before, and I would never do anyone any harm." He was groveling so low to the ground now that his forehead was touching the dirt, and I could barely hear what he had to say at the end because it was mixed in with his sobs.

I couldn't believe what I was hearing. The lengths Pac had gone to—and was still going to—was unbelievable. It was obvious he'd been planning something for a long time.

Fear was beginning to prickle up the back of my neck. Fear that he had Jill and was using her for another part of his plan.

Sandy was the first of us to speak up. "What was my turtle's name?"

We all turned to look at her in shock. Turtle? What in the world?

"Sandy, when have you ever had a turtle?" Mom asked.

She didn't answer, only kept staring at Pac, who looked back at her with a blank look. If there was someone who didn't know the answer to something, he would be it.

"He doesn't know," she said, then she turned and walked away, changing into her wolf and running back home.

"I . . . I . . ." Tears were running down the man's face. "I don't know what she's asking of me."

"None of us do, but clearly she's sure you're not Pac," Dad said.

"I'm not! That's what I've been trying to tell you all. I never even saw his face, so I couldn't point him out to you either."

"What?" Dad roared. "How is that even possible?"

"We signed up to the experiment online and received bottles in the mail. That was it."

"You're telling me you drank some liquid without being aware of what it was, and from someone you'd never met?" Jacob said.

"No. I work in a lab, so I had the items tested for poison. There were no traces of it. I've had no side effects, and the smell has lured females to me, so I'd say it was a win-win—until now that is."

"You never thought to question why someone would be

making something that would change your smell?" Brandon asked.

He shrugged. "I just thought it was another one of those sale gimmicks, and my buddy had been nagging me that I wasn't brave enough to do a dare. I wanted to prove him wrong," he finished in a whisper.

This time I heard a few growls beside me, including my own. Our family didn't tolerate bullies.

"Not much of a friend if he made you do something like that," Mom said.

Dad put an arm around Mom, and she let him keep it there, even though I could tell she was still mad at him because he hadn't told her about Pac.

"I believe you," I said.

"How? This story is ridiculous," Brandon said.

"Jill said the Pac she knew was called Rich, and he was a talented plastic surgeon who also dabbled in science projects on the side. She said their home would sometimes smell like gardenias, and she'd have no idea where it was coming from because she didn't think he'd be home. She also said he'd have odd men coming by randomly, and she'd help from time to time with packaging up bottles of liquid and adding labels to them explaining recommended dosage."

"And you never thought it important to tell us this when you mentioned you found Pac?" Dad said, now standing next to me.

"Why would I tell you? It's not like you told us what Pac had done to Sandy. She had to tell us herself. And what about the time you told all of us that you had taken care of him, but really, because you loved Pac so much, you just told him to run away instead, never thinking that he'd come back for vengeance and hurt our family again."

"That's enough!" Mom said. She had one hand on Dad's arm, which I knew would only hold him back for so long.

"That's enough," Mom repeated in a quieter tone, now coming to stand between me and Dad. "We are a family. We deal with problems together." Mom paused. "Luc, why did you come today?"

I took a deep breath. "My mate is in trouble, and I know it has something to do with Pac, who we think is her ex. He's up to something, and now she's missing."

"How do we know this so-called mate of yours is real?" Dad said.

Mom turned to give him a glare, and I felt my brothers close in behind me. It felt good to know they had my back in case Dad got really mad.

"Theodore McCullough!" Mom announced. "You think your son would have the balls to come home and face you and lie to your face about finding a mate? After the way you treated him after Kit? He's your son, and you love him. You don't want to admit it, but he's your son! Your son, Theodore!" Mom had been pushing her finger into his chest throughout her whole speech, and Dad was cornered into a tree trunk at this point, staring down at the woman who was half his size but had such a strong hold over him. I hadn't heard Mom use his full name in a long time, so we knew she was pissed.

Dad launched off the tree and tried to pull some authority back. "I only want to make sure how serious the boy is this time. We don't want a repeat." He glared at me. "Besides, I know of Jill."

"What?" Mom and I said together.

"Of course, I do. If one of my boys is smitten, I know. I know everything. If any of you think you can hide things from me, think again."

I was boiling inside now.

"I had a scout look into Jill and follow her," he now added. He held up a hand to stop me from talking. "He wasn't with her all the time, which is why he wasn't there when she was taken. He couldn't get too close because it was raining, and there was no one else around to block him from being seen. And"—he held up a hand to placate me, clearly aware I was seeing red—"I was only watching her because Miti is missing too. Yes, Luc, I do care about my own mother. And as callous as you might think I am, I must do dishonorable things sometimes to keep this family safe. One day you'll understand."

A low rumble was forming at the base of my chest, and all I wanted to do was run head first into Dad. My brothers, however, each had a hand on me, preventing me from doing so. I could tell they were upset at what Dad was saying right now too. I highly doubted I'd ever be like him.

"Miti went missing very soon after your Jill moved in. There's something connected there, and as much as you want your mate back, I want my mother back too," Dad added.

Mom had let go of Dad and now had her arms around him. They leaned toward each other in a way that made me ache. My mate was missing, and I felt like half of my heart had been cut away with her.

Thankfully, Brandon was able to put some words together. "Let's go talk to that scout you had. Maybe he's learned something new."

"Rocco is not here at the moment. Go home and wait; we will meet you there."

"I can't wait!" I protested.

"You're going to have to!" Dad yelled back.

Mom came to stand between us again. "We need to deal with him first," Mom said, pointing at the human. "I promise nothing bad is going to happen to him. Right, Theo?" She gave Dad such a stare that he only huffed and nodded his head before turning and stalking away.

As soon as we got back to our complex, Brandon sped up and sprinted toward the main entrance. We all stared after him in shock as we followed behind.

We could hear screaming as we got closer to my room. Then we ran faster but stopped as soon as we saw who it was.

Becca came charging toward me with her hands out. It would have been easy to stop her and hold her at arm's length, especially with Brandon coming up behind her, but I didn't. I let her pummel me. Her hands were everywhere at once, hitting my chest, my shoulders, and even my face a couple of times. I couldn't hear everything she was screaming at me; I was just trying to block her attack. Brandon was able to get her off me after a few seconds, and I stood up, her eyes shooting daggers at me.

"Hi, Becca."

She spat at me and crossed her arms across her chest. "I know you have her here. Where is she? Do you have her locked up in your room again? Ray called me and said Jill never showed up to work. She said you came by looking for her, but I think it's all a ruse." She took a deep breath, and her words were less rushed, but her tone was no less forceful as she continued, "I knew you liked her. I even told Jill it wasn't like you to stand her up. That being Brandon's brother, you were an upstanding citizen and would treat her differently than her ex did."

I growled at the mention of Rich. "And how did he treat her?"

"He'd do the same as what you did—lock her in their room for days, never letting her out unless she was with him. He'd dress her up like a doll so she would look good on his arm, but he wouldn't pay even an ounce of attention to her. She'd get pummeled by him if she didn't do what he said. I was the only one he allowed to call her, and even then, we weren't allowed to talk about much. She was basically under house arrest and his own personal slave." She was crying by this time, and Brandon had his arms around her, helping her stay upright.

The rest of us looked at Becca in horror. How could anyone do this to another? My hands were bunched into fists, and it was only the knowledge that I needed all my energy to find Rich that kept me from taking my rage out on them.

Becca whirled on me suddenly and said, "We have to call the police." She was pulling out her phone when Brandon grabbed it and put it in his back pocket.

"I'm sorry, Becca, but we can't." He was holding his hands in front of him, trying to keep her from getting her phone back as he backed up.

"Why are you doing this, Brandon? My friend is missing! You of all people know how much I care about her!"

Brandon seemed to decide that the best thing to do wasn't to keep backing away from her. Instead, he enveloped her in a hug. I watched in horror, hoping Becca didn't reach the phone and dial the police. If the police got involved, there would be more questions than we could explain. Thankfully, Becca resorted to pounding on Brandon's chest while sobbing instead. I could hear the comforting words he was saying into her ears—we all could—and I wished Jill was here so I could do the same.

All that kept playing in my mind were Becca's words about what Jill had gone through with Rich. No wonder she'd been pissed at me for holding her in my home while we searched for Rich. The guy would pay. He would pay big time.

JILL

I TRIED to sleep but failed miserably. There was some straw in the corner I had pulled together to make two makeshift beds. I tried to entice Miti onto one, but she wouldn't budge. At one point her eyes shot open and looked right into mine. I couldn't look away. It looked like the whole world was behind those eyes, trying to tell me something I couldn't understand. But somehow, regardless of her crazy behavior, her presence seemed to calm me instead of scaring me more, and I decided to sit as close to her as possible.

"I have to change," she suddenly announced, and not for the first time.

I opened my eyes and saw her looking at me. "What do you have to change?" I whispered back.

"I have to change."

She looked so sad and earnest. I wanted to help her, but I didn't know what she needed. Then her eyes closed. It appeared it was the end of the conversation.

I closed my eyes and tried to will myself to sleep. I would survive longer if I could ignore everything around me. Yet sleep remained elusive, just like my wish to be free of Rich.

Even though Rich hadn't come to see me yet, I knew it was only a matter of time. The guards made up for his absence. Every once in a while they would throw something at the cage to scare the living daylights out of us. Usually, that was just me, as Miti seemed too consumed in her own worries to notice. They would laugh raucously, slamming their hand on the table, and at one point I heard one of them fall out of their seat. I rejoiced when he fell, hoping he'd hurt himself, but the guard got right back up and continued playing cards like nothing had happened.

For the hundredth time my mind wandered to Rich and what he'd do to me. Did he actually love me? Or was he just mad that he lost a possession? What the guard said about him having his heart broken echoed through my mind. This was what Rich did to me—he made me doubt myself and feel guilty about my actions and hunger for freedom until I agreed to whatever he wanted me to do. I had many memories of him yelling at me, then changing his attitude on a dime to the sweetest person anyone could meet. Those emotional swings still made my mind whirl. I couldn't deal with that again, and I never ever wanted to see him again.

I could feel my heart rate increasing at the thought of him touching me again. My breath was coming in short spurts, and I could feel tears forming at the edge of my eyes.

A hand crept on top of mine and squeezed. A sense of warmth and love followed, seeping into my body. I opened my eyes to see Miti looking at me, this time with clear eyes. Eyes with understanding, as if she knew what I was going through. How that was possible, I had no idea, but I would take any help I could get.

"It's time for me to shift," she said in a low voice.

"What do you mean?" I whispered back.

"It's time I took some action to help Luc."

I gasped, hope charging through me. "You remember Luc? Do you remember what happened to you?"

"I love Luc," she said, ignoring my question.

"Yeah, he seems like a good man."

"He loves you too."

"What?" The word was louder than expected. One guard yelled for me to be quiet, and in a lower voice I said, "How would you know?"

"I know."

"But how?"

"Luc is my grandson. We are connected."

"He's your grandson?" I repeated. She was very different from Bubbie.

Instead of answering my question, she said, "Luc is a good boy. He's the man for you. He will take good care of you, I promise."

I pulled my hand from hers. "You can't promise something like that."

"I can."

Why was I having this conversation with someone I barely knew? I barely knew Luc too.

"Trust me," Miti now said. "I will set us free, and you will run to find Luc."

"You're going to set us free?" I repeated. Maybe she was crazy. But then again, there was freedom in crazy. Especially with what was coming. *And we are going to be in a world of hurt when Rich shows up.*

Her hand reached up to my face and cradled my cheek. "You are safe with me. Luc is on his way, I know it."

"How—?"

"No more questions. I must concentrate as I need all my strength. I wish I wasn't so old. You be ready when I give the signal."

"What—?"

"Let me be now, child." Her hand left my face, and her eyes closed, and I knew there was no getting through to her anymore. I was stuck in a cell with a lady who was losing her faculties and claimed to be Luc's other grandmother. She was nice enough to Luc when I saw them together, but they seemed more cordial than loving compared to Bubbie and Luc. How would Miti know Luc loved me? Infatuated I could believe, but love?

LUC

I WAS PACING back and forth in the living room. I knew Rocco was still enroute and would be here soon, but Dad and Dredge should be here by now. *Screw waiting!* I turned and began striding to the door when Rocco came in.

"What took you so long?" I demanded, walking right up to him.

He pushed me aside and went to the fridge. Opening the door, he perused the contents, ignoring my question and the fact that all of us were staring at him.

I shoved him away and closed the fridge, standing in front of the door so Rocco had no choice but to look straight at me. Bloodshot eyes looked back at me with indifference.

"I don't answer to you," he mumbled, pushing me aside and reopening the fridge.

"Who cares who you answer to! My friend is missing, and you're withholding information!" Becca yelled, stomping over as if she was going to pummel him.

I was about to back her up when Brandon put a hand on both of us. "Dad is here."

I turned to see Dad and Dredge coming through the door.

Rocco immediately let go of whatever he was about to pull out of the fridge and stood at attention. I had to give it to him; he was the perfect soldier. No wonder Dad trusted him more than me.

Dad glanced at Becca for a second before turning to Brandon with a questioning look, but he didn't say anything. He then turned back to Rocco and took charge. "Rocco, what have you found?"

"Pac's smell is at a bunch of locations. There's a warehouse by the water and an apartment downtown near the hospital."

"That's probably the guy who we found already," Dredge said.

Rocco nodded. "Most likely. There's also the guy who works the Ferris wheel at the carnival in town, and the ice cream guy who walks his cart through the park every day at two o'clock."

"Where is this all going?" I growled.

"None of them are Pac," Rocco said.

"What do you mean?" I said, lunging for him.

Dredge grabbed me and held me back. I tried to fight him off, but Brandon, Jacob, and Bruno came and stood by me too. Even Damon and Brent surrounded me.

"Let him finish. Then we'll know where to go," Brandon said.

I wasn't going to fight all my brothers, and with Dad staring me down, I simmered down.

But Becca wasn't having any of it. "This is ridiculous. I'm not waiting around while all of you wait for him to get to the point. I'm going out to search for Jill." She stomped out of the room.

Brandon's eyes followed her out, but he stayed put, not letting me move an inch from where I was standing.

Rocco continued with a nod from Dad. "I questioned all of them. They all said the same thing the first guy said. They were given something to change their scent, and they all smell like Pac. None of them know anything else."

"They might just be very good actors," I huffed.

"You're the one who told us Jill said Rich was a guy who was capable of this. Now you're—" Dredge started.

"No, I just want something that I can go on. It's been almost a whole day. Jill could be—" I couldn't say it. I didn't want to believe that Rich was hurting her.

All my muscles constricted. I was beginning to see red again. Now that Becca was out of the room, I stopped holding myself back. I felt a bunch of hands hold me down as I swung at whoever I could reach. I started to change, and it was at that moment when my mind was completely wolf when I heard it —a voice was calling me from far away. I stilled, then noticed Brandon and Dredge had changed too. The others circled us, boxing us in. I willed myself to calm down in the hopes they would relax and let me go, but mostly I did it to concentrate on the voice in my mind.

It was a woman's voice—an older woman's voice that was raspy and tired. I made out my name and realized with a start that I hadn't heard her voice in my head in a long time. We'd seen each other every day up until . . . a week ago. I felt sad that I hadn't realized it had been that long. She would disappear for days but never a week, always to come back not remembering where she had been.

"Miti," I said in my mind, and apparently Brandon and Dredge heard me too. I saw them transform back into humans to explain to the others what I had said.

The circle loosened, and Dad walked toward me. He kneeled down and looked me in the eye. "What did you say?"

I transformed back into a human and told him, "Miti."

"Where is she?" he growled.

"Somewhere in a dark cell. She's with my mate."

Dad's eyes widened, and I could tell there was no need for

me to fight my way through anymore. I took advantage of the situation and walked toward the door.

"Which location are you headed to first?" Brandon called after me.

"The apartment by the hospital," I said, already halfway to the elevator.

I heard the others dividing up the locations to search. Dad was giving instructions on finding underground openings. Pac was a tricky one. I'd make sure Dad wasn't going to let him get away again.

JILL

I WAS SITTING in the corner, rocking back and forth, with tears falling down my face. I couldn't believe this was happening again. If Rich wanted to break me down before coming to see me, it was working. I was diving back into old habits—hiding away, experiencing feelings of defeat, and thinking of ways I could comply so that the beating he would soon deliver wouldn't be that bad, if there ever was such a thing.

I felt a hand on my face, and I looked up to see Miti looking at me with clear, bright eyes. "It's time."

"What are we doing?" I whispered. My level of hope was running so low I didn't think I could do whatever she wanted me to do.

"I need you to persuade them to open the door."

"What?" I gasped. "They won't even let us out to pee. How am I going to get them to open up the door?"

"You will think of a way. Dig deep, Jill."

Those eyes would not lift from me, but one thing registered in my mind. "Do you remember me?"

"Of course, sweetheart. You're the reason my Luc is smiling again."

I gaped at her. "How do you know? You've only just met me."

"It only took me one look at you on the day you arrived for me to know you're the one for him. And Luc and I have a connection."

"A connection?" It wasn't the first time she'd said that. "Like you can talk to him?"

"Yes."

I just stared at her, trying to compute what she was telling me, but it didn't make any sense. "How?"

"Not something for you to worry about now. Just know he's coming. But we need to get out first so he can find us."

Then another thought came, and as Miti was actually coherent this time, I had an opportunity to ask her. "Why are you here, Miti? Why is Rich interested in you?"

"He wanted you. He thought he could steal your keys from me, but he doesn't know I don't give things up easily. I will never hurt my family for anyone," she said with determination. "And you are now family."

"I—"

"Need to find a way for them to open the door. Believe in yourself, Jill. The cell is all in your mind. You have the willpower to escape if you put your mind to it."

Her hand was on mine, rubbing the back of it and sending warmth to my heart. Her touch made me feel loved, cared for, safe. Hope bloomed, and somehow, I started believing I really could do this. All I had to do was think of a solution . . . and I soon found that solution at my fingertips!

I gave Miti's hand a squeeze and sent her a soft smile. Seeing the expression on my face, she let go of my hand. Determined, I looked around the cell, searching the dim interior. My gaze landed on the rib bones the guards had thrown at us over the past day. If I remembered the second guard correctly, he was easily provoked, and I had a bet he wanted to please Rich. A plan started forming in my mind.

I looked at Miti and said, "Here's what we're going to do."

"Dwayne, come here," Miti said to one of the guards, standing at the door with her hands gripping the bars.

"Old lady, leave us alone!" Dwayne bellowed, burping up whatever they had just eaten.

I grimaced at the smell that would no doubt come our way in a few seconds. I was standing behind Miti in the dark, wondering if Dwayne would take the bait.

"I'm tired of sharing a cell with this girl! I deserve my own cell!" Miti yelled.

"Shut up, old woman!"

She raised her hand, which was filled with a bunch of the bones the guards had thrown at us, and started flinging some at them. I had to say I was impressed at her aim, as the first handful hit their mark, landing right on their faces.

"Why you—!" the second guard roared.

"Come and get me!" Miti taunted, continuing to throw the bones.

Dwayne, however, seemed to have more control and intercepted the second guard when he was about to come over. "She'll run out of steam soon. Sit down."

We knew this might happen, so Miti went to plan B. She backed up and grabbed my hair. "I will start pulling strands of hair from this girl's head if you don't come this instant."

A pause followed her threat, but I knew what was going through their heads. Rich would want nothing short of perfection when he got me. Even one missing strand would send him over the edge.

"Don't touch her," the second guard said, now standing up to show how intimidating he was. Dwayne tried to push him down again, but he shoved him aside.

Miti reached over and plucked a strand of hair from my head. "One at a time," she taunted. "That's all it'll take until she's bald as a plucked chicken." She took a small bunch of hair this time and pulled hard. I couldn't help crying out. "Or I could do it all at once so all you're left with is a broken girl," Miti finished with a cackle.

We had talked about carrying the threat through, but I'd hoped it wouldn't come to that. The suddenness of it surprised me, and I screamed at the sudden pain, but the sight of my hair in Miti's hand and the guards' sudden hitched breathing made me hopeful.

Sure enough, the second guard came running to our door before Dwayne could catch him. He lunged through the bars to grab Miti, but she moved so fast his hands grasped thin air.

How in the world could a woman this old move so fast?

Miti pulled my hair once more, and again a chunk of hair ended up in her hand. The second guard started growling. Before Dwayne could stop him, he had opened the door. The next few minutes happened in a blur. I backed up against the wall as I watched Miti transform. She was lowering to the floor, fur protruding out of her skin. Her face elongated next, and before I knew it, a wolf was standing in front of me, lips pulled back, teeth barred.

I was frozen in place. What in the world had I gotten into? What was I looking at? This couldn't be happening. Dwayne and the second guard were unprepared for what they were seeing, too, and I could hear them screaming as the wolf charged.

The only thought that kept running through my head was thank goodness it was dark; I didn't want to see the scene in front of me in great detail. The sound of limbs being torn and the screams cutting the air were chilling. The smell of death followed, then silence permeated the blackness.

I was breathing so hard that at first I didn't notice the wolf was standing right in front of me. My chest was rising and falling so fast I couldn't suck in enough air or get a coherent thought through my brain. The wolf came closer, and all I could do was stare back and hope she wouldn't tear me apart as well. Then she dropped her muzzle close to my hand. I froze.

A scream escaped me when the wolf licked the back of my hand. She then used her nose to nudge me before turning and trotting a few steps. She looked back, as if beckoning for me to follow. I was still frozen in place, unable to move, fear holding me rooted to the spot.

Seeing that I wasn't going to follow her, she ran out of the cage and down the hall. There came the sound of a door opening, followed by a bright light shining down the hallway. I heard shouts then, among voices wondering what was going on. The wolf didn't hesitate. She ran after them, and I soon heard the sound of men screaming and more limbs tearing.

Silence once again ensued, and the smell of fresh blood permeated my senses. Somehow, I'd started breathing again. I realized I had to get out here. No one had come down to investigate the cell, and it remained open, beckoning me to make a run for it. I started venturing out of the cell, careful to keep my eyes averted from the ground. I followed the light toward the door and was about to look around the corner when I heard growling and whining coming from the other side. Fear once again held me in place. My heart was pounding so hard I could feel the blood throbbing in my temples.

I wasn't going anywhere. I slumped to the floor, cowering in a ball. I hoped I wouldn't be the next to die.

LUC

Miti's thoughts came in strong as soon as I reached the hospital. The apartment Rocco had mentioned was close by, and I headed in that direction, driving faster when I felt my connection with Miti grow stronger.

When I reached the building, Rich's scent was so powerful I didn't stop to think. I transformed in a rush, crashing through the entrance to the lobby. I followed the screams and sounds of carnage echoing down the hallway until I ran into Miti.

We both transformed and held onto each other.

"I'm so glad you're okay," I said, holding her close. "Dad is very worried about you."

"Your dad will be just fine. Your mate is waiting."

"Thank you, Miti."

"Luc," she said, putting her hand on my face. "She will be traumatized. Treat her gently."

I laughed dryly. "I think that's saying it lightly. I have a lot of explaining to do."

Miti nodded, then ran off, probably to find Dad or cause

more mischief, and I followed the sound of Jill's heartbeat until I reached the door that led down into the dark.

"Jill?"

All that answered was a soft sobbing sound, and my heart broke at the thought that Jill might not be receptive to me after this. I wished I'd found her before Rich had gotten his hands on her, and that I could have spared her from all this trauma. I would have to do everything in my power to support her through this, because one thing was certain—she was my everything, and I couldn't lose her.

With that promise residing in my mind, I slipped into the darkness and immediately saw her crumpled on the floor. I slowly approached and touched Jill's arm. She flinched and looked up with startled eyes.

"Luc." My name came out in a sob.

My resolve broke. Without thinking, I crushed her to me. Another sob escaped her lips as she collapsed into my arms. I picked her up and ran out of there before anyone else could surprise us.

JILL

I WOKE up in my own bed with the sun shining through my window. I sighed happily, realizing what I'd been dreaming of was just a nightmare. Groaning, I turned to see what time it was, only to scream when Luc came striding through my bedroom door.

He ran to my side. "Are you okay?" he said, putting down the tray of food he had brought in with him.

"I'm okay," I said, trying to catch my breath. Then I whispered, "It wasn't a nightmare, was it?"

"No, it wasn't," he said in a somber voice, sitting down next to me and pulling me into his side.

I welcomed his warmth until memories of last night slowly started to seep in. I pushed Luc away when I remembered what I'd witnessed—all the screaming, the sound of limbs tearing, the blood, and most especially the creature I'd seen. I started shaking as the details flooded in. I looked at Luc, feeling my face leaching of color. "Miti! She's . . . she's a . . ."

"Wolf. Yes, we all are." His arm loosened around me as he pulled back, watching my face closely.

The first thought to cross my mind was that I was

saddened at the loss of his touch. It left me confused because we hadn't known each other that long. But then the words he'd said seeped in, and my eyes locked on Luc's. His were a bright golden blaze.

His voice came out low. "My family descends from a long line of wolf shifters. It's why we live out here in the woods. It's why you'll always be safe if I have anything to say about it." He took a deep breath, and his eyes shifted back to their normal shade of brown. "I'd like to show you what that means if you're okay with that."

"Show me?" I whispered. I was having a hard time computing what he was saying.

"Let the girl rest first!" Miti announced, coming to stand in the doorway. She was leaning on a cane, bandages covering her arms and face.

"Oh my goodness, Miti!" I said, standing up and reaching for her.

"Sit down, dear girl. I'm just fine. I've been through worse."

Luc snorted, and I looked at him, but he just winked at me and whispered, "I'll tell you another time."

Miti shuffled to the other side of the bed. We made to help her, but the look she gave us made us stay put while she grunted and maneuvered her body until she was sitting on the bed next to us. "I told you to treat her gently," she said, giving Luc a stern look.

"He is!" I said, hoping Miti wasn't about to get mad at him. If anything, Luc's presence in the room was exactly what I needed.

"What she's saying is I shouldn't have jumped right into wanting to show you how I can transform," he explained.

"I . . ." Then I stopped. I wasn't so sure about what was going on and what I wanted. Did I really want to see him transform into a wolf? I still didn't quite believe I'd saw what

I saw with Miti, but then what else explained all the death that followed in her wake? Miti had changed into a wolf before my eyes . . . and she had talked of changing for a long time before that. The evidence was stacked in favor of Miti being a wolf shifter. But Luc . . . ? He had just said he was one too . . . and Miti had claimed that she wanted to protect her family. Did that mean that Luc and his brothers and everyone else in his family—including Bubbie—were all wolf shifters?

My mouth dropped open.

As if she could see the thoughts in my mind, Miti said, "It's okay, Jill. You are family. There is time. What is important now is that you rest and heal."

"You saved me," I said, looking at Miti. That was one truth I could cope with right now.

"Yes, but I couldn't have done it without you. You saved yourself too," she said, pointing to my chest. "You believed in yourself. Why else would you have let me pull out your hair?"

"You pulled out her hair?" Luc asked with an expression of horror.

"Well, pulling out *my* hair wouldn't have made such a big impression on the guards," Miti said, giving Luc a confused look.

This made me laugh. The absurdness of our situation, and Miti talking about pulling out my hair, added in with Luc's sudden fear that Miti would do it again, made me bubble over. I laughed and laughed till all I could do was lean against Luc. Finally, when I'd calmed down, a contented sigh came out of me.

"I know you have a lot of questions for us, Jill, but now is not the time to ask," Miti said. "You need to eat. Luc, grab the soup you brought in."

Luc, looking as though he had no idea what else to do, did what Miti said and held the soup bowl for me while I ate.

It wasn't until I was almost done that I looked over at Miti to ask how she was, only to find she had started snoring.

"I do have a question I would like answered now," I whispered to Luc.

His face softened, and he turned to put the empty soup bowl on the bedside table before facing me again. "Yes, what is it?"

I glanced at Miti. "How is she not more hurt?"

"The doctor they thought was Pac is now the doctor at Dad's compound. He bandaged her up like new."

I shook my head. "No, I mean how is she not *more* hurt? I thought she would be in the hospital after what she did."

He looked me up and down and said pointedly, "Well, how are you not more hurt and in the hospital?"

"Very true," I laughed. "I just know she was a lot more . . . physical than I was. I thought she'd have broken bones and such."

"She did." After a pause, he added, "A wolf heals a lot faster than a human."

I waited for him to say more, but Miti's snoring was all we heard for the next minute. Images of Miti transforming flitted through my mind, but before I could follow my train of thought, Luc said, "It's time to rest. Why don't you take a nap, and I'll bring you more food when you wake up?"

I smiled as he tucked me back into bed. "I could get used to this," I confessed, feeling my eyes begin to feel heavy.

"I hope you do," Luc whispered.

I heard him go to the other side of the bed and lift Miti up before exiting the room. Deciding that I'd take their advice on the rest, I closed my eyes and let my mind go blank. I could worry about what Luc had said another time.

Becca came by the next morning and showered me with chocolate and wine before crawling into bed with me and watching reruns of Friends.

"Luc told me that when he and the others went searching for me, Brandon went searching for you instead."

"Yeah, he did." Becca blushed, and I was happy to see her have that kind of reaction to Brandon's chivalry. "He found me pretty quickly after I left. I was just wandering the streets, yelling your name. I was so frantic and scared for you, Jill. I was worried that you . . ." A sob came out of her, and I held her tight as we both cried.

"All is well. I'm good," I reminded her.

"He wouldn't let me keep looking for you. He told me the cavalry had set out to search for you, and they would do a much better job at finding you than me screaming at the top of my lungs going about without a clue as to where you were."

She paused to take another sip of her wine before continuing, "He took me to his apartment and held me until we heard that Luc had found you. I started bawling. Oh, Jill." She squeezed me tighter. "I don't know what I'd do if you were gone forever."

"I'm here, though. I'm right here."

We didn't say much else the rest of that morning, just munched on food and watched television. In the afternoon, Becca asked, "What happened last night? Are you okay to talk about it?"

I thought about how much I should share with her, but besides Miti's transformation, which I still wasn't sure was real, I didn't want to tell Becca all the gory details. No one needed to live through that if they didn't have to.

"I was walking to work when I was kidnapped," I said simply, then stopped for a second as I thought about the connotations behind that word.

"Are you okay?" Becca whispered. "We don't have to talk about it."

"No, I just realized saying the word kidnapped out loud really makes a difference in how I think of the situation. It makes it real, you know? That probably doesn't make any sense."

"I'm a lawyer, remember? Words have meaning, and they're even stronger when spoken aloud."

I looked at Becca and nodded. "You understand."

"I do."

I gave her a hug. "I'm so lucky to have you as a friend."

"We're family. We're all each other have. So, what happened after they took you?"

"I was locked in a cell with Miti. They kidnapped her while trying to take the keys to my apartment."

"They came to the apartment?" Becca looked horrified.

"Yes . . . I hadn't made that connection."

"You were a bit traumatized at the time, so I don't blame you. Do you know if they got your keys?"

"You know what? I don't know. I never asked." I sighed. There was so much I could have done.

"Don't do that."

"Do what?"

"That sigh," Becca said firmly. "You're second-guessing yourself, and I won't have it."

"Oh," I laughed. "You know me too well."

"I sure do, and I know you're blaming yourself right now for not doing more." To distract me, she continued with her questioning. "How did you two escape?"

This was the part where I fudged the story. Luc had told me last night about Rocco's surveillance results, and how he had decided to be the one to go to the apartment by the hospital. So I said to Becca, "Not much else to it. Luc came and saved the day."

"Oh yeah, Brandon said Luc was headed to the apartment. I'm so glad he did!"

"Yeah, he knocked out the guards and was able to get us out of there before anyone else showed up." That sounded plausible, right? She didn't need to know that there were multiple guards and that a wolf shifter saved the day.

"Thank goodness. I'm so glad you're okay."

"Me too." And I was especially glad she went for that ending.

I had been thinking on and off about what I had seen in the cell. My bruises and torn-out hair were proof that I was really there, that last night had actually happened. So that meant Miti's transformation was real too, right? And what Luc had said—that they were all family—meant that he and the rest of them were wolf shifters too. Now I'd had some time to digest the news, it felt surreal. But I couldn't deny what I'd seen in that cell, or how brawny the men in Luc's family were, including the way they behaved with their growling and protective behavior. My eyes widened at the truth—his family *were* wolf shifters!

Becca had started the next episode of Friends, and I decided that now was not the time to dive into more memories of last night. There was always tomorrow to think on that further.

JILL

I stayed in bed for one more day, but on the third day, I was getting so antsy that Luc and Julian, the human doctor the pack had adopted, agreed that I was okay to go back to work.

Ray was so happy to see me, and I had to say the feeling was mutual. We made floral arrangements while chatting the whole morning. I couldn't have been happier.

During my lunch break, I walked over to my creek, as I liked to call it. I sat on the log and listened to the birds and the tinkling stream as it flowed by. A sharp snap came from across the stream, startling me. I opened my eyes to see the same wolf from before looking back at me. His white fur was glistening in the light, and the black tips of his ears were pointed toward me. He lay down with his paws crossed in front of him, his brown eyes warm and welcoming . . . much like a man I knew. He looked like a sphinx, regal and powerful.

"I was wondering if I'd see you again," I said. "A lot has happened since we last met."

One of his ears twitched, as if in acknowledgment.

"I met a guy." I smiled at this. "He looks macho, but he's really sweet."

At this, the wolf lowered his head, his eyes half closed, as if he were laughing.

A lot had happened since I left Rich, and meeting a guy who could make me smile was not one of the things I had considered possible. And yet . . .

It was time to address the question in my mind. I looked the wolf in the eye and said slowly, "You're him, aren't you?"

Nothing happened at first. We just looked at each other until he stood on all four paws. Then, right before my eyes, the wolf transformed into Luc. "My Luc," a voice inside my mind said, and I liked the sound of that. He walked across the stream and kneeled in front of me.

For some reason, I wasn't scared. Warmth seeped into my body where his hands touched mine, and a sense of calm washed over me. "You saved me too," I whispered.

His face was solemn. "And I always will. We're mates; destined to be together."

I stared at him in wonder. "How do you even know that?"

He smiled. "I'm comfortable with you unlike anyone else. Not to mention I'm not complete without you."

That warm feeling spread into my chest, flooding it with hope and promise. "I feel that too."

"You know deep down inside that we're meant to be together, Jill. You're my mate, and wolves mate for life."

"For life . . . ?"

He raised a hand and brushed a few strands of hair away from my face. His thumb brushed my cheek, and I leaned into him. "You're my everything, Jill, and I will spend whatever time it takes to prove it to you."

He leaned in and kissed me, his lips soft and gentle. I melted into his arms, letting him pull me in close. His touch was tender, like nothing I had ever experienced. I felt safe and cherished.

"I'm glad to see you two are finally together," announced a voice.

We jumped apart to see Miti smiling at us.

"Grandma!" Luc cried.

"Miti!" I said at the same time.

"It's good to know I can still sneak up on you, my good boy," Miti said with a laugh and danced in a circle.

I was the first to recover. "Miti, how are you healed already? You had some really bad injuries."

She turned to show me how well she was. "It's one of the benefits of being a wolf, my dear. We heal a lot faster. I'll also let you in on a little secret." She came within a foot of us. "I also have an infinite number of lives," she confessed with a wink, and headed back toward town, dancing all the way.

Luc rolled his eyes. "Don't pay her any mind," he said. "No one really understands her, but we all know that she loves us and will take care of us with her life, if needed. Just as she did for you."

"But I'm—"

"Family. For ever and always. You are one of us now, Jill."

I sighed at that. It was a contented sigh, and I leaned further into Luc, cherishing this moment and his warmth and protection. He felt like home, and with him by my side, I knew I could face whatever was thrown at me—even a crazed, possessive ex who had kidnapped me.

I knew Rich was still out there, and a part of me still wanted to hide forever so that he couldn't hurt me anymore, but the feel and smell of Luc next to me reminded me of how far I had come. I was healing, and with Luc by my side, Rich would never control me again.

EPILOGUE

JILL

"BUBBIE, this duck soup is to die for," Becca said after tilting her bowl up to get the very last drop.

Bubbie laughed. "It's good to see you two eating so wholeheartedly. Have as much as you want; I can always make more."

"But we're so full now," I said, rubbing my stomach. "I think I'll have to call Luc to carry me home."

Bubbie laughed all the way back to her kitchen.

I'd been coming once a week to help her with her cooking. She'd been teaching me some of her family recipes. It was so nice to learn more of my culture, something I never got to dive into after Mom passed away.

"You look happy," Becca said.

"I am." I sighed. "I really am."

It had been a month since the escape from that awful cell. After Luc saved me, his dad had immediately brought a team in to clean up the mess at the apartment so the police were none the wiser about the slaughter that had gone on. All the police had been told was that I'd been kidnapped and locked in the cell until they came and saved me.

The real Pac was still at large, apparently no longer working at the hospital. I spent a couple of weeks in fear that he was hiding behind every corner and would jump out at me at any second, but nothing ever happened.

I had moved in with Luc, and I now felt even safer. I was free to go wherever I wanted, but given Pac was still out there, Luc said he couldn't breathe if he didn't have someone watching me. One of the pack was always on duty—at a discrete distance, of course. The tracking no longer grated on my nerves; I knew it came from a good place.

"You're glowing and have that far-away look on your face again," Becca said, looking over her teacup at me.

I laughed. "I was just thinking about how lucky I am to have you and Luc and his whole family in my life."

"You deserve it."

"You do too, Becca," I said, reaching over and giving her hand a squeeze. "Brandon didn't leave your side for almost the whole first week after I came back."

She flushed. "I know. I had to tell him to give me some space."

"Which it looked like he had a hard time doing," I pointed out with a smile.

"I know! I eventually had to drive back to the city to have some alone time."

I watched Becca twirl her spoon in her empty bowl, lost in her thoughts, until Bubbie came back out with a tapioca ball dessert.

After finishing mine, I said, "I think you should try again with Brandon, Becca. Don't give up on him." I wanted to tell her that Brandon was acting like she was his mate. If that was the case, there was no way Brandon wasn't into her.

But I couldn't say any of that without explaining what I knew about Brandon's family. Becca would freak out if she knew they were wolf shifters. Besides, that information was

Brandon's to share, not mine. All I could do was encourage my friend to not give up on him. There was bound to be something that would make the man see what a catch he had.

But then Becca said, "I think it's a lost cause, Jill, but thank you for your support."

"Oh, Becca—"

Bubbie came in again to get our dishes and saw we were teary-eyed. "Is that how my food makes you react? I thought bringing you dessert would make you girls smile again."

We laughed.

"No, Bubbie, just boy trouble," I said.

"Ah. Let's not have boys be our problem right now then. Come in and help me make some green onion cookies. That will have your boys eating right out of your hands."

"I'm game for that," Becca said, getting out of her seat.

I smiled as I followed along behind her. I would make sure Becca had the best chance she could get.

Thank you for reading Jill and Luc's story. The family saga doesn't end here. Continue The McCullough Pack series with Becca and Brandon in *Loved by the Wolf*. Continue reading for a sample or **visit this link to start reading**.

nolalibarr.com/books

If you enjoyed the story, a brief review is always helpful on Amazon, BookBub, and Goodreads. It'll help new readers discover these books.

Sneak Peek

Loved by the Wolf
The McCullough Pack Book 2

Brandon

Becca really was the most beautiful girl, both inside and out. That was cheesy but so true. I'd give her the world if I could have her, but what we had right now—a mutual friendship— was all I could allow.

Her hand grazed mine—for the third time—and each time we touched it felt like a lightning bolt shot right through to my core. I held my breath, hoping it wasn't obvious how much her touch affected me.

"Sorry, I'm looking for Rich's paperwork," Becca said, shuffling some papers next to me.

A huff came out of her. I looked up from my work, my gaze latching onto her pouty red lips. They matched the red hair cascading down her back. My fingers itched to reach out and touch those fiery strands. I twirled my pen to avoid balling my hand up into a fist.

Oblivious to my thoughts, Becca asked, "Have you finalized the paperwork on Rich yet? I can't find it anywhere."

"Almost." Darn, I thought she'd trust me to get it done and not worry about it.

"Almost? It's been a month since Jill left."

"Yeah, I know. I just need to get Rich himself to sign it."

"I thought—"

"He's been hard to get ahold of." Not a complete lie. He'd called a couple of times, and I had ignored them. I was still fuming from the knowledge that Rich was Pac. I'd now wronged two of the women I loved the most—my sister and Becca. This time, my hands did ball into fists, because the memory of Sandy getting attacked by Pac while she was looking after me as a pup flashed through my mind. That image was soon followed by the remembered sound of my nose breaking when Pac knocked me out. I felt my eyes close, and my head started drooping into my hands.

"Brandon!"

Becca's small, warm hands squeezed my shoulders, immediately erasing the memories, and I looked up into her startling, bright hazel eyes. "I'm okay." I put on my best smile to wipe the worry off her face. "I'm just tired."

"Okay." But she didn't sound sure about that and lingered next to me a minute more.

The smell of the soap she used to wash her hair wafted into my senses, and my wolf reared up to claim her. I pushed him back down, clenching my fists under the table. *No!* I shouted at him through our connection. *Don't scare her!*

"Maybe we should call it a night?" Becca suggested.

"We've barely done anything, though."

"But you look like a mess. Are you sure you're okay?"

"Yes. Let's just get this brief done."

She laughed. That laugh could melt the hardest heart. Though, if you asked Becca, my heart was unmeltable. What she didn't know was that she'd melted mine the first day I met her—when she dropped ice cream on my brand new Ferragamo's. We were inseparable since then, but I'd always made a point to not give her any reason to think I wanted to be anything more than friends. Which meant touching her arm tonight in the hallway was a mistake. I could still feel her skin burning into mine, but I squashed it down. It wasn't worth the pain. I couldn't tell Becca how I felt, or how I would fail her just like I failed Sandy—just like I failed my family when they depended on me. I wasn't the man for her. She deserved so much more.

"Something's going on with you, Brandon," she said, poking me in the chest, "and I'm going to get to the bottom of it. You"—poke—"just"—poke—"watch"—poke—"me."

I'd watch you all day long and then some. A deep growl threatened to come out, but I subdued it. My wolf had been extra active lately, especially since Luc claimed Jill for his own. I was next in line to claim my own mate, and my wolf was eager for me to do so.

I pushed my wolf deep down inside me. I would let it out later tonight when it could run for as long as it wanted. I would tire it out until it couldn't think anymore. It was the only way.

I grabbed Becca's finger, which was still on my chest, and planted a light kiss on the pad.

Wait! Why in the world did I just kiss her hand? Maybe she didn't notice? But, on looking into her eyes, I saw her pupils had dilated. Looking for a quick way out, I placed her finger on the paper we were working on. "I need your signature here so we can move on," I said swiftly.

"Ugh. Way to break the moment."

I'm the best at that. Just ask anyone. The words remained unspoken; the best way forward was ignorance of what I'd just done.

We worked for a couple more hours until we were both satisfied. I was lucky to have her as a partner. She was the hardest working attorney in the office as far as I was concerned. The best to look at too. I shook my head at that thought. Her brain was what I liked, not her body. Though, her body was perfect. Just the right size for me.

I groaned inwardly. It wasn't this hard to control my thoughts a month ago. What was happening? Working with Becca had never been an issue. I was satisfied I got to see her almost every day, and on the days I didn't see her, we kept in touch via text. I was her protector. Nothing else.

Lately, though, my thoughts had started going sideways. It started with that darn ball. She had been so excited when she learned my family used to throw masquerade balls. So excited that she begged me to get tickets. Luc was still laughing at me for making actual tickets, knowing full well our family were always invited and no one needed tickets.

"Okay, I think we're done working for the night," Becca announced with a sigh. She sat back in her chair and stretched her arms over her head.

The action caused her shirt to lift just a smidge, and it was enough for me to see a line of her alabaster skin. It was all I could do to not reach out and run my hands along that strip of skin. I forced my mind back to her comment. "Are you sure?"

"Yeah," she said, her chair landing back on all four legs. "We've done what we can for tonight. I have to get a couple of signatures, but that's it."

"Well then, I guess it's time for me to go."

"You could stay a bit longer and we could chat," she suggested. The look in her eyes was pleading, and I knew I had to leave as soon as possible or I'd fall right into their depths.

"No, we have an early morning tomorrow. You should get some rest."

"Right."

I almost changed my mind at the look of disappointment that crossed her face, but knowing I couldn't lead her on, I stuck to my morals before they fled. "Goodnight, Becca. I'll see you tomorrow."

"Alright, see you tomorrow."

She didn't look at me as I walked out the door, and when I caught a glimpse of her as I shut it after me, I saw her head going down to the table as a big sigh escaped her mouth.

Visit This Link to continue reading Loved by the Wolf.
nolalibarr.com/books

Free Book Offer

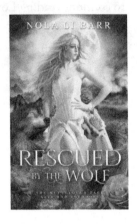

Meet the parents that started the McCullough Pack. Receive a FREE copy of *Rescued by the Wolf* when you join Nola's newsletter. Be the first to know about new releases and giveaways.

newsletter.nolalibarr.com/mcculloughpack

More From Nola

Paranormal Romance

McCullough Pack

Rescued by the Wolf (Alia and Theodore)
Saved by the Wolf (Jill and Luc)
Loved by the Wolf (Becca and Brandon)
Adored by the Wolf (Millie and Jacob)
Protected by the Wolf (Lira and Bruno)
Admired by the Wolf (Sandy and Thomas)
Healed by the Wolf (Jasmine and Dredge)
Freed by the Wolf (Ray and Stewart)

Contemporary Romance

Skyline Mansion Series

Forbidden Blossom
Hidden Blossom
Secret Blossom
Family Blossom

Companion Stories to the Skyline Mansion Series

Summer of New Love

Summer of Second Chances
Summer of My Dreams
Winter of Beginnings

About the Author

Nola Li Barr writes sweet family saga romances. Both in contemporary and paranormal settings. She writes stories she would love to read herself and loves exploring family dynamics with her characters. In the hopes of sharing her stories with her kids sooner than later, her romances are always sweet with a happily ever after. When she's not writing she can be found reading, making photo books, and navigating the path of motherhood.

www.nolalibarr.com
@nolalibarr